Scott grinned. 'I didn't get a wink of sleep all last night,' he mused, 'because I was regretting that I hadn't taken you up on your invitation——'

'I didn't issue any invitations,' Jill snapped.

He didn't seem to hear. 'I was wrong last night,' he said, very softly. 'I do want to make love to you again.'

He was six feet from her, but the warmth of his gaze was so strong that her skin was aching as if he were stroking it.

'That's your misfortune, Scott,' she said shakily.

NO PLACE LIKE HOME

Graham was kind and gentle, and Kaye had agreed to marry him. Everything should have been perfect, except she seemed to be spending more time with Brendan McKenna, her estate agent, than with her fiancé. And the search for her dream house was continuing for a very long time . . .

JUST A NORMAL MARRIAGE

Shauna McCoy's mother, Jessica, was too self-centred to be a good mother to her young daughter, Mandy. The logical solution was that Shauna should look after her half-sister. But Jessica wouldn't hear of it unless Shauna was married, and the only man willing to take on both Shauna and Mandy just wasn't Shauna's type at all . . .

SHADES OF YESTERDAY

Courtney would never have asked old Nate Winslow for help unless she'd had to, and it irked her that his son Jeff seemed to think she was an unsavoury scrounger. After all, Nate owed her something—hadn't her mother said so? She didn't know what it was, but she was sure it must be important . . .

LET ME COUNT THE WAYS

Sara Prentiss had found a haven in Chandler College, and in Olivia Reynolds the mother she'd longed for. Then famous thriller writer Adam Merrill arrived—and found a mystery right in the middle of Sara's peaceful little world . . .

ONCE AND FOR ALWAYS

BY

LEIGH MICHAELS

MILLS & BOON LIMITED
ETON HOUSE 18-24 PARADISE ROAD
RICHMOND SURREY TW9 1SR

*First published in Great Britain 1989
by Mills & Boon Limited*

© Leigh Michaels 1989

*Australian copyright 1989
Philippine copyright 1989
This edition 1989*

ISBN 0 263 76310 2

*Set in Plantin 11 on 11 pt.
05 8907 50288*

Typeset in Great Britain by JCL Graphics, Bristol

Made and Printed in Great Britain

CHAPTER ONE

IT was hot, and the air-conditioning in the heavily loaded van hadn't worked right since they had picked it up at the rental place in Chicago that morning. That was enough to make everybody grumpy, even without Joe Niemann chain-smoking cigars and the assistant cameraman singing along with the hard-rock music that streamed from the tape-deck . . .

It was not a good omen for a week's work on location, Jill Donovan thought, when the crew couldn't even get to the site without being at each other's throats. I must be crazy to have signed on for a project like this, she thought. I'm going to be spending a whole week of July on location in the middle of a cornfield in Iowa, sitting on an all-terrain vehicle and smiling for the camera, when I could have stayed in New York——

She sighed. It pays the rent, Donovan, she reminded herself. Not that she was in desperate need of work; she had always made good money in her modelling career. But, on the other hand, there had never been people lining up at her agency to ask Jill Donovan to model designer dresses and jewels for *Vogue*, either. Her jobs had been less glamorous ones—like posing for advertising photos of all-terrain vehicles, she reminded herself.

She pushed the button that let her seat lean back, and from behind her came a howl. 'Donovan, are you trying to cripple me? You almost smashed my knee!'

She put the seat upright. 'Sorry, Gareth.'

'You could think ahead a little. I nearly pulled a muscle dodging you.'

He sounded like a whiney child, Jill thought. That was the biggest problem with male models, she concluded: they were so ridiculously protective of their precious skins that they had little energy left to be interested in anything else.

'Why is it that pretty women never have any brains?' Gareth complained.

'Thanks for the compliment,' Jill said crisply. She had known Gareth Morris for years; in fact, she had dated him a few times, but it hadn't taken long for her to become disenchanted with the petty personality that lay behind the handsome face. Gareth was certainly good-looking, but his attitudes about women were strictly chauvinist. On the plane from New York to Chicago, he had passed the time by making slyly off-colour comments to the flight attendants. Jill, who had been sitting beside him, had not appreciated his wit.

'Oh,' he said, on a note of discovery. 'You're just jealous because I don't find you particularly attractive any more.'

She longed to point out to him that he hadn't been the one who had called a halt to their dates; she was the one who had suddenly been too busy. Had the egomaniac really not noticed?

'Well,' he said philosophically, 'I suppose there won't be much else of interest to do in this hick town we're going to—what's the name of it again?'

Joe Niemann, who was the advertising executive in charge of producing this new campaign for North Star's all-terrain vehicles, puffed a particularly noxious cloud of cigar smoke into the van and said, 'Springhill.'

'I didn't know there were any hills in Iowa,' Gareth said.

'Maybe it was just wishful thinking when they named it,' the assistant cameraman volunteered.

Gareth had lost interest. He leaned across the seat and studied Jill's profile. 'What about it, Donovan? We might as well kill time together—have a little fun. I doubt there will be anybody interesting among the natives.'

And that, Jill told herself, was the other problem with male models; they were so convinced of their attractiveness that they believed every woman they met was eager to fall into bed . . .

'And give Springhill a chance to see how the beautiful people behave?' Jill said, a little cynically.

'Why not?' Gareth shrugged. 'No commitments, of course.'

'I know. You wouldn't want me sitting on your door-step when you get back to New York. Thanks, Gareth, but I'm afraid I'll be too busy to have time to party with you.'

Gareth frowned. 'Doing what? We can't work at night, you know. What do you plan to do with your time?'

Jill thought about telling him that she couldn't wait to see how her crossword puzzle book turned out, but she thought Gareth was probably too dense to see the insult.

'Leave her alone, Gareth.' The head cameraman didn't even turn his head, he just kept staring out of the window.

'What's it to you, Danny?' Gareth challenged.

'I'm interested because we've got one week to shoot this ad, and that doesn't leave time to wait while your bruises heal.'

Gareth recoiled. 'Bruises?' he shrieked. 'Are you threatening me?'

'Nope. But if you bother Jill, she may just punch you in the eye.' Danny turned then, and winked at Jill, who smiled back. She liked Danny Mitchell, and even though she didn't really need defending, he was a dear to stand up for her. She could even forgive him for getting her into this ridiculous assignment. A magazine advertising campaign for a sort of three-wheeled motorcycle, running through a cornfield in the middle of Iowa . . . Whose crazy idea had this been, anyway?

Gareth settled into his seat with a little flounce. 'Joe, would you mind putting out that cigar?' he called peevishly. 'It's terrible for my skin to be exposed to smoke. And it's making Donovan here look absolutely haggard. Once a woman gets past a certain age, you know——'

Jill thought grimly, You may not have to wait long for those bruises, Gareth. How in heaven's name could I ever have dated the man?

Joe Niemann, who had ignored the entire exchange while he puffed gently at his cigar, took it from between his lips. Instead of crushing it out, however, he waved it like a pointer. 'I give you Springhill,' he said. 'Your patience has been rewarded.'

The irony in his tone was drowned by the applause of the other five people in the van. Jill pulled the curtain back from the window and stared out across a little valley where a town nestled along the banks of a twisting river. There were hills, she saw, and plenty of them; the town crept up the sides of some, while others formed a sort of natural basin, their wooded slopes gently rolling against the horizon. At the moment, there was not a cornfield in sight.

As pretty as a picture-book, Jill thought. And just as dull. Once, in the heat of anger, she had declared that nothing could ever get her to set foot in the state of Iowa. Now here she was.

But not for long, she reflected. Surely a week wasn't long enough for a case of terminal boredom to set in. Though, if it came to that, she had had plenty of practice at dealing with boredom in her seven years as a model. The resulting photographs might look glamorous, but the process, Jill had long ago discovered, usually wasn't.

Seven years, she mused. It didn't seem possible that it had been so long since she had gone to New York City, to the bright lights that had been beckoning to her since she was a child. Seven long years——

She had been a little older than the average beginning model when she had been discovered, but then she had never really considered modelling as a career. There were so many other jobs, other challenges—anything was possible in the city.

Once into the field, though, she had quickly found that the rewards could be great for a young woman willing to work hard. And Jill could work very hard indeed. There had been no commitment important enough, no opportunity intriguing enough, no entertainment fascinating enough to interfere with her work. Certainly there had been no man appealing enough to make her give it up.

And that devotion to work was explanation enough for her presence in a van crammed with crew and cameras and props, pulling a trailer loaded with two all-terrain vehicles through a landscape lined with cornfields. It had been a good many years since she had made that passionate vow never to enter the state.

In any case, it had been a silly, childish thing to say, even in the midst of a quarrel . . .

She shifted uneasily in her seat at the memory. She had thought she had forgotten all that, buried it in the long-dead past. Well, it didn't matter, that was all, she told herself firmly. She would do her job the best she could and move on, and what difference did it make which state she was in?

The van pulled up under the broad canopy over the entrance to a sprawling motel complex, and the crew released a sigh of relief, almost in unison.

Jill zipped up her tote bag and settled her broad-brimmed hat over the knot of black hair at the crown of her head. She hoped there was no problem with checking in; all she wanted right now was a shower and a chance to stretch out in a quiet room.

'The Journey's End Motel?' Gareth said with a snort. 'What a dumb name!'

Preferably, Jill thought dreamily, a room at least four blocks away from Gareth Morris . . .

'Journey's End?' he went on. 'Who in their right minds would consider this to be the best place on earth?'

'A lot of very nice people,' Danny Mitchell told him. 'And a few stinkers. Pretty much like every other place you've been.'

'You're such a philosopher,' Jill murmured as Danny helped her down from the van. He shrugged, and she turned away with a smile.

The motel doors opened and suddenly the van seemed to be surrounded by men and women, all wearing forest-green blazers with gold emblems on the pockets. For an instant, Jill wondered if they'd landed in the middle of a convention. Then one of the blazers grabbed her hand and shook it painfully hard.

'As a member of the Diplomats' Club,' he announced, 'I'd like to welcome you to Springhill. We're a division of the Chamber of Commerce, and we always like to make our visitors feel welcome—'

Jill retrieved her hand and cautiously flexed her fingers. *Welcome* was hardly the word, she thought; *besieged* might be more like it. Another green blazer had buttonholed Danny, she saw; Joe Niemann was surrounded by them. Two more blazers were studying the bright red paint of the pair of all-terrain vehicles on the trailer.

'Looks just like a souped-up motorcycle to me,' one of them said, shaking his head.

I couldn't agree more, Jill thought. She saw another blazer hovering and clasped her fingers together in an operatic gesture in an attempt to ward off a handshake. 'It is so nice of you to greet us,' she began.

She was being watched. The hair on the back of her neck seemed to curl up in apprehension. That's odd, she thought, half-consciously. I haven't felt like this since I was a teenager—clumsy and embarrassed——

Jill Donovan had long ago come to terms with the fact that wherever she went, men were apt to be looking. She might not meet the strict interpretation of beauty, but she had the kind of face and figure that men of all ages seemed to find arresting, and she had stopped feeling awkward about it years ago. Sometimes she enjoyed the frankly admiring appraisals that came her way. More often, she simply ignored them. Once in a while, when an evaluation of her face and figure went on a bit too long for comfort, she would return the favour and stare the offending male into a shamed retreat. But she hadn't felt this way in years, as if she were being stripped for a man's private enjoyment.

She turned her head casually, trying to get a glimpse of the man who was so crude in his appraisal. Only a hick would behave like that, she thought contemptuously. Perhaps Gareth was right after all.

Then, across the sea of green coats, she saw a tall man who wasn't wearing green, a man with dark brown hair with a rebellious wave. He wasn't watching her—he was talking to Joe Niemann instead—and abruptly she forgot to look for the man whose stare had made her so uncomfortable.

No, she thought. It can't be.

Jill had never tried mind-expanding drugs, but she had been told that sometimes they made colours turn into symphonies and single words drag out for minutes. That was what it felt like in the aeons-long instant when she stood under the canopy at the Journey's End Motel and stared at the man who looked like Scott Richards' identical twin. Scott, the man who was the reason she had made that theatrical vow never to set foot inside Iowa . . . Except it wasn't a twin, she knew. It was Scott.

Springhill, she thought desperately, and searched her memory. It still didn't set off any alarms in her mind. She had never given a thought to Scott Richards, when Danny had told her about this job. There had been no reason to think of him, of course; all that was long dead and buried. But to find herself face to face with him now, here——

Had Scott even told her which small town in Iowa he had grown up in? Surely she couldn't have forgotten!

I don't think he ever mentioned the name, she decided. And I certainly didn't ask him to point it out on a map. I had no interest in his past. It was only the future that mattered, and my future was in the city, not in some town scarcely big enough to need a set of traffic lights. And Scott's future was in New York, too—at least, I thought it was. Funny, that two people can spend so much time together, and share so many things, and yet know so little about each other.

She stole another look. He had turned towards her, and instead of a profile she could now see all of his face. It was thinner than she remembered, and there was a hint of silver in the dark hair at his temples. He's too young for that, she thought, with a pang of sadness. He's only thirty—just a year older than I am.

Another blazer-wearer captured her hand and squeezed. 'We're so glad,' a booming voice from near her shoulder level announced, 'that North Star's new advertising campaign will be produced right here in Springhill.'

'Save it for the welcoming party tonight,' a calm voice told him. 'There'll be plenty of time.'

Jill didn't look up. She didn't have to. His voice hadn't changed. It still had that slightly husky timbre, the vibrant softness that was like an intimate hand stroking her skin. I wonder if he still knows how to laugh, she thought absently.

'Miss Donovan——'

She looked at him then, surprise brimming in her wide green eyes. She had to look a good six inches up at him, and that was something that didn't happen to Jill Donovan very often. Her eyes were almost on a level with the cleft in his chin.

So it was going to be formal, was it? she thought. As if they had never met before, as if they had never shared—— Her heart seemed to skip a beat as she remembered the things they had shared.

'Mr Richards,' she said, and didn't realise, until

she saw Joe Niemann at Scott's elbow, with his eyebrows lifting in surprise, that she should have waited for the introduction. Joe never hesitated to ask uncomfortable questions, she thought. She just hoped he waited till the Diplomats all went away.

She singled out her two-suiter from the pile of luggage that the two bellboys were unloading from the top of the van. Scott picked it up; she pulled her hand away quickly, but she could feel the warmth of his skin even though their fingers hadn't quite brushed.

He carried it into the lobby, where yet another bellboy took over. 'In case you're wondering,' he said, 'when Joe made the arrangements to shoot this campaign in Springhill, he didn't submit a list of his crew to the Chamber of Commerce.'

So Scott had been just as surprised as she was, she thought. And less than pleasantly, he seemed to be implying. She raised her perfectly arched eyebrows and said coolly, 'After all, why should he?'

'No reason at all, of course. I'll see you at the welcoming party tonight,' Scott said. 'There are a lot of people who are anxious to meet you.'

Jill nodded, too preoccupied to take offence at his half amused, half cynical tone. The bellboy settled her into her room and went off, pocketing his tip with satisfaction, and Jill closed the door behind him and went to open the curtains. But she didn't see the swimming-pool that lay in the courtyard under her window, its water a trembling sheet of silver under the brilliant sun. She was still seeing the handle of her suitcase, with Scott's long strong fingers curved around it——

And the heavy gold wedding ring he wore.

*   *   *

It should have been no surprise, of course, that Scott had married. He wanted to marry you, Jill, she reminded herself.

She closed her eyes, and suddenly she was no longer in the motel, but back in that little sitting-room in her sorority house, the room where they had had their first and final quarrel. She could even remember the pattern of the wallpaper—an old-fashioned print of pink roses clambering up shadowed trellises.

She hadn't been expecting him to come that evening, she remembered, and she had been in a frantic hurry to rush down to him. 'You shouldn't do this, you know,' one of her sorority sisters had warned as she started down the stairs. 'You'll let him think that he owns you, and once a man believes he's got a permanent hold on you, there's no end to what he'll demand.'

The advice had been almost prophetic, Jill thought, for permanence was exactly what was on Scott Richards' mind that night. Not that he had demanded, precisely. The poor fool had actually expected that she would jump at his offer, that she would be flattered . . .

There was a knock on the motel-room door, and Jill's heart jolted. Had he waited for the Diplomats to scatter, and then come here?

Don't be ridiculous, she told herself. He as much as told you downstairs that he was going to treat it as if it never happened, and that would be the smart thing for you to do, too. You're here to do a job, Jill.

She pulled the door open. Joe Niemann was in the hall, still puffing on his cigar. 'Just checking to be sure you're comfortable,' he said.

'You can come in,' she told him, 'if you leave that filthy weed outside. Gareth's right about smoke, you know, even if he did insult me with the way he said it. It's bad for the skin.'

The director looked mournfully at his long cigar, then sighed and stubbed it out in a hall ashtray. Jill stopped blocking the door and let him in.

'How's the room?' Joe asked.

For the first time, she looked around. It was typical of mass-construction motels; two double beds, with the headboards permanently attached to the wall; a small desk, a table with two chairs, a tiny bathroom, a television set mounted to the wall. The colour scheme was neutral, the art on the walls was mass-produced but inoffensive, the whole place was squeaky clean and nearly devoid of personality.

She shrugged. 'It's all right, I guess. Better than some I've stayed in. At least it looks as if there's a good light to read by.' She sat down on the foot of one of the beds and started to take the pins out of her hair.

'It's only for a week,' said Joe.

'Do you really think we can shoot it so quickly?'

'On the budget we've got, we'll have to. North Star isn't being terribly generous. But I don't see any reason why we can't do it; they only need one good photo, and if we take back half a dozen for them to choose from, the company will be thrilled.'

It made her feel better; it wasn't that she didn't trust Joe Niemann's reputation, but his confidence was reassuring.

'Why do you ask?' he went on. 'Have you got a hot date in New York next week?'

Jill smiled unwillingly. 'Not exactly, but——'

'That must mean you've already got cornfield claustrophobia. I'm getting to be expert on the subject, because Gareth's got a particularly bad case.'

'Gareth is an idiot.' Jill tossed her head, sending

blue-black ripples of hair to her waist, and started to brush rhythmically. 'He may have a gorgeous body, but he's strictly absent-without-leave above the eyebrows.'

Joe chuckled. 'That's why I was so glad when Danny said you would take this job,' he confided. 'I'll have my hands full restraining Gareth, and I won't have time to worry about you.'

Was that a warning? Jill wondered. 'If he's such a problem, why use him?'

'Because the people at North Star think he's got a gorgeous body.' Joe rose. 'The party starts at eight—it's sort of a buffet dinner and reception, I guess, to let all the locals see that we don't have two heads. They're having it here at the motel for our convenience.'

She didn't look at him, and she kept her voice carefully casual. 'Do you mind if I just sit it out, Joe? Going to a party tonight to be inspected by the whole population of Springhill isn't my idea of fun.'

'So don't go,' said Joe, with a shrug. 'It won't keep me awake at nights. But I'll warn you—if you don't show up, it will just increase the curiosity level. Most of these people have never seen a real live New York model, you know.'

She eyed him warily, the brush suspended in mid-air. 'Do you mean they're likely to be hanging around while we're working, too?'

'Well, there is a public road within fifty yards of where we'll be shooting, so I can't exactly lock the doors to keep them away. But I don't think that will be much of a problem, really, once they get over the novelty.'

'And the sooner they see us all, the sooner they'll get over it?'

'Something like that. I think you'd be better off to get the public bit over with right away. Then they'll leave you alone. But do as you like.' He reached into his pocket. 'Here's the schedule for tomorrow.'

Jill looked at it and groaned. 'You want to be on the site by seven?'

'Soft morning light looks better out there, and it's going to take a while to set up the equipment before we can even start to shoot.' He grinned. 'So don't worry about being trapped at the party all night, because I'll send you to bed early.' He stopped in the hallway to retrieve the remains of his cigar from the ashtray. 'By the way, Jill,' he said, 'in case you're trying to hide from Scott Richards, staying in your room isn't the smartest way to do it.' Then he was gone.

Hide? The mere idea made her furious. She wasn't hiding. There was nothing to hide from. She was just tired from the long, hot drive, and she had a headache because of that blasted music.

But if Joe suspected that she was trying to avoid Scott, she realised, Scott might think the same thing. And she certainly didn't want him to get the idea that eight whole years later she might still be carrying a torch for him—or a grudge, either, if it came to that.

'All right, I'll go to the damned party,' she told herself irritably, and went to take a shower. 'I'll be charming and clever and urbane if it kills me, and I will not give Scott Richards the satisfaction of thinking I'm hiding from him!'

So Scott had got married. Well, she told herself, wounds heal, and I'm glad that he didn't let my rejection turn him into a hermit. He's too nice a guy to spend his life alone.

Scott had been a charming young man—talented,

thoughtful, brilliant, and an almost perfect gentleman, she reflected. He would make a good husband and provider, assuming that the woman in question wanted to live in Springhill, Iowa.

Jill shivered. It's fine for some people, she thought, but I just couldn't bear to be buried alive in a little town like this. Why Scott couldn't understand that—

But he had refused even to try to comprehend her reasons. He was such a traditional man, as she had discovered that night when he had asked her to marry him and to go home with him. It was one of the things, she reflected, that she had never suspected about him, one of the important things that had never been discussed. She had assumed that when he got his degree in advertising, he would be off to work in one of the big agencies in Los Angeles or New York—he certainly had the talent, and the drive. Perhaps some day there would be an agency of his own . . . And instead, all the while, he had planned to come back here, to this crossroads of nowhere.

But perhaps that wasn't quite fair, she reminded herself. It hadn't been part of Scott's plans for his father to have that massive heart attack, in the autumn of Scott's senior year at the university. But there could have been other answers, things that would have solved the problem without Scott giving up his whole future—and hers, as well.

Instead, he had rushed back home to step into his father's shoes in the family hardware business. Hardware, of all things, Jill thought. It made her sick just to think of his talent mildewing while he sold bolts and wire and plumbing parts.

Eight long years, and here he still was. Was his father still alive, despite that heart condition, and refusing to let Scott go? Or was it Scott's own idea to stay here now?

Had he ever really wanted to live in the fast lane? It was the first time Jill had ever considered that possibility, but she vaguely remembered that it had been she who did the talking about how wonderful life would be in the city. Scott had smiled, and kissed her, and turned her attention to other things . . .

I wonder, she thought, if even then he was certain that I'd put my dreams aside and come with him. I had no idea he was such a chauvinist, expecting a woman to give up everything for her man.

Well, obviously he had found a woman who agreed with him. She wondered, pettishly, how long he had been married. Had he found another girl on the rebound? Or had his wounded heart taken years to heal?

'Perhaps he didn't even really want to marry me at all,' she said, against the roar of the water. 'Perhaps he just wanted to be married before he came back here, and he didn't much care who it was.'

She wondered what his wife was like. A small-town girl, or a city import, as Jill would have been? Was she pretty, or just ordinary? Did she, perhaps, look a bit like Jill herself? And did she know that there had been another woman in his life?

Jill wondered with morbid interest if that was why Scott had addressed her so formally this afternoon, cutting off any possibility of an embarrassing public reunion. Just what would happen if Scott Richards' wife was to find out that once upon a time he had proposed marriage to the woman whose face could be seen this month on the cover of *Today's Woman*? It might be a bit difficult for him to explain now, if he had neglected to tell her long ago.

Jill turned the shower off and smiled at herself in the steamy mirror. It was a mischievous smile. 'It would be rather fun to watch,' she mused. 'Perhaps I should make sure she knows.'

Tonight's party might not be boring after all, she decided.

She took particular care with her make-up. She didn't use a lot of it—she never wore much except when the cameras demanded it—but the right shades, carefully applied, could change her from an elegant society type to a sultry siren who might have been spotted on any street corner. Tonight she deliberately chose the All-American-girl look, wide-eyed and natural. Any man in the room would swear that she wasn't wearing a speck of anything on her face. The women would know better, but most of them wouldn't have the vaguest idea how she had done it.

She pulled her hair straight back from her face and looped it into a sort of double ponytail. A few loose tendrils around her face softened the severity of the style and helped to emphasise the strong planes of her face, the prominent cheekbones, the huge eyes, the firm chin.

Not bad for a woman of twenty-nine, she told the mirror, no matter what Gareth Morris thought. She was not over the hill. A woman could model as long as she wanted, if she was willing to be flexible about her jobs, and if she didn't let her body go to ruin.

She hadn't brought many clothes; how much could it take, she had thought, for a week of rural rustication? Her entire wardrobe fitted into a tenth of the tiny wardrobe, and she looked at it with dissatisfaction. There was a crate of sports clothes for the photo sessions, of course, but nothing that she wanted to wear tonight. She thought longingly of a scarlet sequined dress that was hanging in her apartment in New York—that would get everyone's attention. But it wouldn't exactly fit the image she was so carefully creating, so it was just as well she hadn't brought it.

She turned back to her wardrobe with a sigh, and finally settled on a white skirt just a little longer than fashion said was proper this year, topped with a black blouse that was perfectly demure and yet somehow left nothing to the imagination. She added a row of bracelets, a chunky necklace, and earrings, all in a deep strawberry red, stepped into a pair of four-inch heels, and nodded at herself approvingly in the mirror.

The banquet room on the motel's lower level opened on to the pool area, but since the evening had not cooled off much, the glass doors were closed. The water looked inviting, Jill thought. Too bad it wasn't a bit more private; she would enjoy a dip just now.

From the sound of things, the entire population of Springhill had turned out. She stood in the doorway for a moment, just looking over the crowd. There were men in suits, in the green blazers of the Diplomats' Club, in jeans. There were women in diamonds and organza cocktail dresses, and ones wearing tennis clothes.

Danny saw her and brought her a glass of spring water. 'Isn't this the damnedest thing you ever saw?' he said. 'I've seen more good character types tonight than I have in a month in the city. I wish I dared to get my camera and just start shooting.'

She saw Scott across the room. He was in a group, and yet somehow he seemed to be alone. Until then, she hadn't realised that she had expected to have no problem identifying his wife; Mrs Richards would of course be the little lady clinging to his arm. But there was no woman nearby who looked like a candidate; the one he was talking to would never see sixty again.

'Checking out the territory, Jill?' said Gareth, with no attempt to be quiet about it. 'You shouldn't have any trouble lining these hicks up—they're standing over there staring as if they've never seen anything quite like you.'

Jill sipped her spring water and looked up at him with a saccharine smile. 'Actually, I thought it was you they were studying, Gareth,' she murmured.

A teenage girl came up to them. 'Are you the model?' she asked Jill. 'You sure don't look like I expected.'

'You're too kind,' Jill said sweetly. She would have liked to grab a face flannel and wipe the mascara off the child's eyelashes.

'I want to be a model,' the girl announced. 'Maybe you can tell me what I should do.'

Learn to walk correctly, Jill thought. Learn to stand up straight. Learn to treat people with respect, instead of as if you're already a super star. 'Perhaps later in the week I can find a few minutes to help you,' she murmured.

There was an amused feminine chuckle beside her. Jill looked down at the woman at her elbow. Something seemed to tickle her memory, and yet there was nothing familiar about this small and somewhat pudgy woman, a good eight inches shorter than Jill and probably twenty pounds heavier. Her face was round, but her eyes were bright, and her amusement was obviously genuine.

'I didn't think you were insensitive,' Gareth accused her. 'Everyone needs a helping hand, Jill.' He turned to the girl. 'I'll be happy to give you some tips,' he said, and the girl fluttered her eyelashes up at him.

Jill watched them irritably as Gareth guided the girl across the room to a private corner. But she saw from the corner of her eye that Joe Niemann hadn't missed the byplay either, so she relaxed. Gareth's conduct certainly wasn't her problem.

The woman standing beside her gestured with her

plate of hors d'oeuvres. 'Apparently,' she said, 'this is why our lives didn't take the same sort of path. I get easily sidetracked by food and drink, while you—my God, Jill, you look wonderful!'

Jill searched her memory frantically. I can't know anybody else in this town, she thought. It would just be too odd——

'You don't recognise me, do you?' the woman said. 'Well, I'm not surprised. I almost didn't come to the party, you know. I was ashamed to have you see me like this. You're more gorgeous than ever, and I'm still trying to lose all the weight I gained while I was pregnant.'

The voice, Jill thought. I know the voice, and the eyes. 'Cassie?' she said. Her voice came out in a sort of squeak. It was just too incredible that one of her sorority sisters should turn up in Springhill too. Of course, it had been a big house, and because Cassie was a couple of years younger than Jill, they had never been really close. But hadn't it been Cassie, that night she had quarrelled with Scott, who had told her never to let a man think he owned her?

'It truly is a small world,' Jill said. 'I had no idea what had happened to you——'

Cassie hadn't stopped talking. 'But Scott made me come,' she said. 'And I'm glad he did. You look wonderful, Jill, and I'd have hated not seeing you again. Can you come and have lunch with me one day?'

And then Jill knew that it was not coincidence that had brought Cassie to Springhill. Cassie was the girl Scott had married.

CHAPTER TWO

SHE swallowed hard. Lunch? Don't be ridiculous, she told herself. And yet there was no real reason why she and Cassie shouldn't have lunch and a good gossip. It was all over long ago, what had been between her and Scott, and it was obviously not bothering Cassie. But——

'I don't know,' said Jill. 'My schedules's going to be unpredictable, I'm afraid.'

Cassie wrinkled her nose in distaste. 'We'll work it out,' she said. 'Maybe if Scott said something to your Mr Niemann——'

'I'll talk to Joe,' Jill said hastily. 'Can I let you know?'

'Of course. I don't need much notice—I've been at home all the time since the baby came.'

Of course, Jill thought. A devoted mother, at home with her child. What a charming picture of domesticity it made—just the sort of pattern Scott had wanted Jill herself to be a part of. 'How old is the baby, Cassie?'

'Well, she's really not a baby any more, she'll be a year old this week. She's talking a bit now, and she's got such a sunny view of the world—— Oh, I'm sorry, Jill. You can't possibly be interested in Jamie's progress.'

'Of course I am.' Cassie seemed to glow a bit when she talked about her little girl, Jill thought, and a tiny sliver of envy nagged at her. Cassie seemed so certain of herself.

'Do you have children of your own?' Cassie asked.

'No—oh, no.'

'I thought you might have kept your name professionally.'

'I've always been too busy to think about getting married.' It was light, easy, casual. Joe Niemann beckoned to her from across the room. Jill nodded at him and said, 'I'll try to arrange some free time this week so we can catch up on everything, Cassie.'

But it was an empty, meaningless promise. Have lunch with Cassie? In Cassie's house? Admire Cassie's daughter—and Scott's? No. It would be far better if she was just too busy.

From the corner of her eye, she could see Scott watching her as she crossed the room to Joe's side. She would have liked to stick her tongue out at him in defiance. Why was he staring at her like that, anyway? Was he hoping that she would fling herself on the floor and throw a tantrum, because he'd had the nerve to marry another woman? Well, if that was what he was expecting, Scott Richards' ego was in for a shock!

She slipped her hand into the crook of Joe Niemann's arm. 'This is the woman's editor of the local newspaper,' he said. 'She'd like to interview you tomorrow, Jill.'

Jill turned on the charm, automatically. 'How nice to meet you.'

Scott was still watching her. It made her furious; he hadn't even come close to her all evening, and he was hovering across the room now as if he was making sure of a quick exit, yet he seemed to think that she had been placed in this room solely for him to stare at. Well, if he wants to play games, Jill thought, I'll show him a few new tricks!

She let her gaze wander over him with slow

thoroughness, from the deep brown of his hair to the well-polished toes of his shoes, and back. He was the picture of the successful small-town businessman, she thought. He was wearing a sports coat the colour of cream-rich coffee; it was pushed back and his hands were in the pockets of his trousers. The clothes fitted him well, making no secret of broad shoulders and powerful legs. It would be a lot more satisfying, Jill thought, if his college-football physique had run to fat by now.

She had every intention of looking him over and then turning away with a disdainful shrug, as if she had concluded he wasn't worth the effort. Instead, she found herself smiling at him, a sultry, come-hither smile. She could have kicked herself for it as soon as she realised what she'd done.

A dull red flush crept up Scott's face, and he turned hastily away. Jill was contented with that. It might not have been quite what she had intended to do, but it was obviously effective.

The newspaper woman looked at Scott's retreating back, and then at Jill. Her eyebrows were raised.

'We're old friends,' Jill said, with a casualness that she knew quite well sounded suspicious. 'Very old friends.' She shook hands and agreed to a time for the interview the next day, and the editor drifted off.

A housewife appeared with one of Jill's magazine covers to be autographed, and by the time she had finished, there was no sign of Scott and Cassie. Jill smothered a small smile and made her excuses too.

But she hadn't waited quite long enough. She had to cross the lobby to reach the stairs to her room, and just as she entered the big reception room, she heard Cassie's voice near the front desk. 'She's always been very pretty, hasn't she?'

Jill drew back into the hallway as a deeper voice replied, 'I suppose so.'

'Scott, you know she's beautiful. Her skin is like porcelain, don't you think?'

'Oh, quite,' said Scott. 'And the rest of her is harder yet.' The heavy door squeaked as it closed behind them, leaving Jill standing, speechless, in the lobby.

So that was what he thought of her. Harder than porcelain, was she? Because she had refused to give up her own dreams to cater to his demands. Well, she thought, he was a pompous, inflated caveman.

No, she decided. Not quite that; he wasn't in the same category with Gareth, who had no respect for women. It was just that Scott had wanted to wrap her up in tissue paper and keep her safely tucked away from the world, so that she didn't have to bother her little head about unimportant things like careers.

Well, Scott Richards could go jump into the river, she thought. He'd got better than he deserved with Cassie, who apparently adored him.

Jill had just finished applying conditioning lotion to her hair and wrapping the entire mess in plastic when the telephone on her bedside table began to ring. She looked at the clock and sighed; obviously Joe had forgotten to issue a do-not-disturb order at the desk. Well, she would have to do it herself. The last thing she needed, on top of a genuine headache, was a telephone ringing at odd hours.

He didn't bother to identify himself, but then there was no need. There was no other voice in the world quite like his, Jill thought. 'I'm in the lounge,' Scott announced. 'Come down and I'll buy you a drink.'

'No, thanks. I'm washing my hair.' It was crisp, but she didn't hang up on him. Much as she hated to admit it, she was curious.

'I could come up to your room, if you'd rather.'

'Absolutely not.' She found herself tightening the belt of her terry robe as if to protect herself.

'I want to talk to you, Jill.'

'I'm amazed. You didn't seem to want to chat earlier this evening.'

'I didn't have anything to say then.'

'So what's on your mind now?' Had he and Cassie quarrelled? The party was long over. There had been plenty of time for a king-sized fight, though Jill frankly couldn't imagine Cassie doing any such thing. Cassie, she thought, was so innocently trusting that she sounded almost naïve.

'Come to the lounge and I'll tell you.'

Jill shifted her grip on the receiver. Conditioner was escaping from her plastic hood and inching in droplets down her neck. 'Why should I go anywhere?' she asked coolly. 'There are only the two of us on the phone. You can say anything you like.'

'If you're not down here in five minutes, I'm coming up.'

'Goodness,' she jeered, 'aren't we domineering? Did you bring a battering ram to use on my door?' He'd probably climb the fire escape and throw a stone through her window if he couldn't talk to her any other way. And given the choice of the bar or her room, there was only one sensible thing to do. But she couldn't quite bring herself to yield.

There was a brief silence, and then, more gently, Scott said, 'Would you please come down, Jill? Just for a few minutes?'

The husky softness of his voice seemed to drag at her senses. With an effort, she kept her tone flippant. 'So your mother did teach you a few manners. Have a Perrier with a twist of lime waiting for me—I'm not planning to stay long.' She put the telephone down with a firm little click and went to rinse the conditioner out of her hair.

He was looking at his watch when she came into the dark little lounge and joined him at the tiny table in the far corner. Her hair was still wet; she had tied it back with a bandanna, and she was wearing jeans and a body-hugging red knitted shirt. She sat down across from him and tipped the green Perrier bottle over her glass, watching the bubbly water hiss against the ice cubes.

'You really were washing your hair?' he said.

'Did you think it was only an excuse?'

'I've heard it before. How many hours a day do you spend on being beautiful?'

In the dim light, she couldn't see the expression in his eyes. But there was no mistaking the cynicism in his voice.

'As many as it takes. That's my profession.'

'Is it taking longer these days?'

'You could have been rude at the party, Scott; you didn't have to make me come down here to listen to insults.'

'Sorry.' He didn't sound as if he meant it. 'I didn't intend it to be an insult, anyway; it was a serious question. I mean, you can't model for ever, can you?'

He took a long swallow from his glass. 'When I left the university,' he said thoughtfully, 'you were majoring in art history and planning a fulfilling career as a museum curator somewhere. Whatever happened to that idea?'

She shrugged. 'I got the chance to do this instead.'

'Did you finish your education?'

'Would you like a copy of my curriculum vitae, Scott? No, I didn't get my degree. I left the unverisity

about a year after you did. I decided that I could
always go back and finish, but the opportunity to
model would only come along once.'

'And you're happy with your job, standing around
day after day like a plastic doll, smiling just right so
that some company can use your anonymous face to
sell their products?' He sounded doubtful.

'It isn't always anonymous,' she pointed out. 'And
it isn't always advertising.'

'Is that what you call a fulfilling career, Jill?'

It irritated her. What made him think it was any of
his business, anyway? 'I'm happy with it. It's good
money, and I work when I like.'

'And you preferred it to marrying me.'

He sounded almost depressed. For a moment she
had to fight down the insane urge to comfort him, to
assure him that it had been no such thing, that if he
had only been sensible—— Then she reminded herself
that he had, after all, married Cassie; that certainly
didn't indicate a broken heart. She straightened her
shoulders and said, firmly, 'Yes, I did. And I'm not
sorry. I absolutely adore living in the city.'

'Yes, I remember how fond you were of cities.' It
was dry. 'The pace, the bustling life-style. The
opportunities and the culture—all the things we small-
town peons miss out on.'

She sipped her water. 'I thought we'd finished this
discussion eight years ago. If that's what you called
me down here to talk about, I think I'll go back to my
room.'

'It wasn't.' But he seemed unwilling to specify what
it was.

Jill sat there for a long moment and looked at him.
Her eyes had finally grown accustomed to the dimness
in the little bar. He had left his coat and tie some-

where, and the open-necked shirt made him look younger, more like the Scott of her college days. The young man who had shared her dreams for the future with the same depth of passion with which he had explored the intimate secrets of her body. At least, that was what she had thought then.

She took too big a drink of the Perrier, and the bubbles burned her throat. She choked a little, and coughed, and had to wipe her eyes. 'So what do you want to talk about, Scott? It's a little dark in here to play chess.'

For a long moment she thought he wasn't even going to answer. 'I didn't think that was the game you had in mind tonight, at the party,' he said, and stared straight through her, over the rim of his glass.

The implication was perfectly clear. He thought she had issued an invitation, and he was eager to take it up.

So the perfect husband had a flaw, she thought. It made her feel just a little sick.

You're a damned romantic, Jill Donovan, she accused herself. Haven't you run into enough married men who cheat, or who would like to cheat with you, to convince you that a faithful one is a very rare species indeed? But somehow, she hadn't expected that sort of behaviour from Scott, the traditionalist.

If this is his idea of respect for marriage vows, she thought, I'm glad it's Cassie and not me who's waiting at home for him, with his little girl. Someone ought to teach this guy a lesson. If I were going to be here for a few weeks, instead of just a few days, I might take on the job.

On the other hand, she thought, it might not take a matter of weeks, and it would be sheer pleasure to teach Scott Richards a lesson that he would never forget . . .

She shrugged. 'Why not?' she said coolly. 'I'll have time on my hands, and there's obviously nothing better to do with it.'

There was an instant of silence. 'I'm flattered. I noticed that you surveyed all the males in the room tonight before you settled on me.'

She shrugged. 'It's habit, I suppose, to look around,' she said, very deliberately.

'To say nothing of your own crew. That's a cute trick, actually, Jill, to be hanging on the arm of one man and at the same instant seducing another one with your smile.'

In her indignation, Jill momentarily forgot herself. 'There is nothing romantic about my association with Joe Niemann,' she snapped.

'I never suggested there was,' Scott said silkily. 'It seems more a matter of cold practicality to me.' He looked at her for a long moment and then picked up his glass and swirled the ice in it. 'And since I am not interested in picking up our torrid little affair where we left off, I thought perhaps I'd better straighten you out before you did more than imply things with smiles across crowded rooms.'

She should have been relieved, for Cassie's sake. She wasn't; she was furious with him for leading her on, for making her look like a fool. 'Then why did you spend the entire evening staring at me?' she challenged. 'You looked like a starving puppy who was waiting to be tossed a bone.'

'I was trying to figure out what I ever saw in you that made me ask you to marry me.'

It was a cold statement of fact, and whether it was true or not, it stung. 'Obviously, you've answered the question to your satisfaction,' Jill said with a shrug.

'It's very simple. I confused a mere physical attraction with something more lasting.'

'Please don't blame me for your mistake.' It was icily polite; she was proud that the bitterness didn't seep through her voice. So, too, had she been confused, thinking that what they shared was a lasting love. Thank heaven, she thought, that his father's heart attack had happened when it did. If he had proposed to her under other circumstances, she might have accepted. And then, when the inevitable happened and he insisted on coming back here, and what they had thought was love died under the strain— She shivered at the idea of the tragedy that would have been, if they had been already married.

'Oh, I'm not blaming you. In fact, I'm grateful. I learned more about making love from you that autumn, Jill—though I'm not sure it's fair to call it that, when there was no love about it. Where did you learn it all?'

From you, she wanted to shriek, but her pride wouldn't allow her. At that instant, she would have said anything that came to mind, no matter how crude, so long as it would make him stop saying these things, stop reminding her of how it had been between them. 'I'm glad you appreciated the lessons, Scott.' She knew she sounded hard and cold, and she didn't care. 'Perhaps you should have had your bride send me a thank-you card on your honeymoon— shame on you for not thinking of it.'

His eyes darkened, and for a split second she was actually frightened of him. Water had condensed on the outside of the Perrier bottle; she drew intricate lines on the table top with it because she was afraid to look at him.

Why did I say that? she asked herself frantically.

I'm not like that, really; I'm not vicious and catty. It's just the shock. But what difference does it make what he thinks about me? she mused. He told Cassie I'm harder than porcelain, and no matter what I said, he would never believe anything else, now. I have my pride, after all. I'm damned if I'm going to let him think I've been wandering around the world dreaming of him for the last eight years.

Scott looked at her for a long time, and then said, reasonably, 'It was over between us eight years ago, Jill, and there's no point in making it a matter of public discussion now.'

She shivered, delicately. 'Why do you think I'd want to make a scene, anyway? I could, you know, and it might be fun. But if you're so concerned about it, why suggest that we meet in the bar?' She reached across the table and rubbed her fingertips sensually against the back of his hand. 'It would be such a shame if anyone got the wrong idea, wouldn't it? A pillar of the community, and a New York model, hiding out in a dark, intimate little bar——'

'We're hardly hiding,' he pointed out.

'And if I were to do this, for instance——' Jill pulled his hand across the table to her, until his palm cupped her cheek, and turned her mouth into it until her lips rested against his lifeline. The contact was like a jolt of electricity, and she had to will herself not to pull back.

'You're not going to quit, are you, Jill?' Scott said calmly. 'All right, have your scene. I suppose I can't blame you; you must not suffer rejection very often.'

She was speechless for an instant, and her hand dropped away from his. 'Listen, Scott, it's only your own gigantic ego that makes you think I'm interested in going to bed with you. All I said was——'

He didn't seem to hear. 'Maybe you should rattle your glass or something,' he suggested. 'The bartender is watching TV at the moment, so you're wasting your time if you don't get his attention.' He didn't pull his hand away; it still lay against her cheek in a kind of challenge, and the warmth of it was like a brand against her skin. She could feel the pulse beating in his fingertips, or was it her own blood flowing crazily through her veins?

She was suddenly, heartily ashamed of herself. Why hadn't she had the dignity simply to say that of course she didn't want to embarrass him or herself—or Cassie—by making a fuss about the past? She could have coldly announced that if he wanted to read hidden meanings into a simple smile he was the fool, not she. She could have put him in his place with icy arrogance and said that she did not wish to lower herself by remembering that brief affair. And then she could have stalked out of the bar with her dignity intact.

Instead, she had confirmed with her behaviour that she was the cold, cynical and catty woman Scott thought she was—harder than porcelain. For what purpose? To drag him down, to make him regret what he had lost? How utterly ridiculous that was!

Cassie might not be a beauty, Jill thought with sudden humility, but she certainly isn't a cat.

And neither am I, she thought. Not really. It's just that he brings out the worst in me.

It was a depressing thought. She pushed the Perrier bottle aside and without a word walked out of the little bar.

Scott caught up with her in the lobby. She didn't look at him; all she wanted to do was get to her room before the tears that were stinging her eyelids could escape.

His hands came to rest on her shoulders, and he turn-

ed her gently to face him. 'You didn't say goodnight,' he
reminded her, but before she could shape the words, his
mouth had found hers, with a sureness that would have
insulted her if she could have thought more clearly, and
if she hadn't been more horrified by her own reaction
than by anything he was doing. She felt as if she was
completely out of control, as if she had suddenly become
a puppet, with Scott manipulating the strings. His hand
cupped her face; his other arm supported her and held
her tightly against the length of his body. Jill relaxed
against him with a little moan and let his tongue probe
gently, insistently. And when he finally released her
mouth, she would have sagged to the floor if he hadn't
kept an arm about her.

Her mind was whirling. 'Why did you do that?' she
demanded hoarsely. Her voice was no more than a harsh
whisper.

He was breathing a little faster than normal, and his
words had a tinge more huskiness than usual. 'You
seemed determined to start people talking about us,' he
pointed out. 'I just thought it might as well be an
interesting rumour. Goodnight, Jill. Sleep well.' His
thumb traced the fullness of her lower lip. If she'd had
any presence of mind left at all she would have slapped
him, but by the time she had gathered her poise, he was
gone.

The night clerk at the motel desk was wide-eyed. Jill
glared him into cowed silence and ducked up the stairs
to her room. She was breathing as if she had just
finished a marathon.

'You're an idiot, Cassie,' she said, and her voice was
harsh in the quietness of the room. 'You're a damned
fool to trust him. And you're a bigger fool for trusting
me.'

No woman with sense fools around with a married

man, she reminded herself. It had long been one of the rules Jill had lived by, and it had served her well. No matter how misunderstood the husband, or how unpleasant his marriage, or how convincing the story he told, a married man was strictly off limits.

To all appearances, Scott Richards was not a misunderstood husband trapped in an unpleasant marriage. And he had not told her any story at all, convincing or otherwise.

But tonight, Jill admitted painfully, if Scott Richards had wanted to come upstairs with her after that devastating kiss, she would have forgotten her rule. She would certainly have thrown common sense to the winds, and she would probably have gone to bed with him.

Common sense, she told herself, was something that had always been in short supply, in her dealings with Scott Richards. She would probably never have met him at all, if she had done the sensible thing and signed up for a course in computers, or business mathematics, or chemistry. But the seminar in classical music appreciation had looked more interesting. And that was how, on the first day of classes in the autumn term of her junior year at university, she had walked into Millard Hall and sat down across the circle of chairs from Scott Richards.

Jill was no stranger to male admiration; she knew an appreciative look when she saw one. What startled her was that after class the brown-haired stranger who had spent the entire hour studying her made no effort to get acquainted. What surprised her even more at the next class meeting was that he came in after her and took the chair across the room, instead of the empty one beside her. He was behaving like no other male she had ever met, and even though she told herself she didn't care, she found her eyes and her thoughts straying from Bach to him all the way through the lecture.

And she was astonished at herself a full week later when she walked into the room and paused beside him. 'May I sit here, or is this seat taken?' she had asked.

He'd looked her over and said, 'I'm not sure.'

'How can you not be sure whether someone is sitting here?'

'Are you as much fun to talk to as you are to look at? Because if you're not, I'd rather you go over there and sit so that I can enjoy looking.'

Any young woman with half a brain, Jill thought, would not only have walked across the room to avoid him, she would have gone out of the door and straight to the registrar's office to switch into another class. Instead, she had sat down beside him, and at the end of the class, he had said, 'Not bad. You can sit with me next time too if you like.'

She had started to fume with irritation at his arrogance, which only seemed to amuse him, and she decided then and there that she would never speak to him again. The next class, she had made sure there were no empty chairs near her; he took a seat across the circle and went back to watching her. After class, he was waiting in the hall. He had bought her a Coke at the student union, and after that she had never looked back.

It was only much later, when she knew him better, that she had recognised the advertising techniques he had used to pique her interest. Yes, she thought, Madison Avenue would have acclaimed Scott Richards as a genius. It was a pity that he had never made it there.

Common sense, Jill thought, staring out at the dark water of the swimming-pool beneath her window. It was something that had been singularly lacking in her younger self. Well, thank heaven she had managed to find a little now. He hadn't invited himself up to her room and even if he had tried, she wouldn't have allowed anything of the kind. Now that the momentary panic was over, she was certain that she would not have yielded to that sort of temptation.

'So stop over-reacting and go to sleep,' she ordered herself. 'You were just in shock at the idea of seeing him again after all these years, that's all. If you'd known that he would be here, you would have been fine. And in any case, you wouldn't have done anything crazy, when it actually came right down to it. Now that's past, you'll be just fine.'

As far as acting crazy, she thought, Scott had behaved even more foolishly than she had, tonight. The idea of grabbing her like that in the lobby, for a madly passionate goodnight kiss! If he didn't want rumours flying, he had certainly done the wrong thing there. Jill almost giggled at the memory of the night clerk's expression as he watched Scott's exit; the man so clearly couldn't wait to tell someone—anyone!—what he had seen.

'Wait till Cassie hears about that,' she muttered. 'I won't have to worry about coming up with an excuse not to go to lunch, that's sure.'

And Cassie would hear. In a town the size of Springhill, half the population would have heard about it by the time the newspapers landed on the porches at dawn. Had Scott been in shock himself? she wondered. He had to have been, or he would never have done anything of the kind. He had to know what the consequences would be.

Jill stared thoughtfully out of the window.

Well, she thought, trying to be cheerful about it, at least everybody will know that he didn't spend the night with me. But I wish he had found some other way to make his point.

CHAPTER THREE

THE cornfield that Joe Niemann had leased as a location for the advertising pictures was nearly ten miles out of town, on a gravelled road. It might have looked more scenic if Jill had been wide awake when they arrived, but as it was she merely groaned in relief when the van pulled off the road and stopped jolting. They were already behind schedule, and it was going to be at least another hour before they needed her, she knew. It would take that long to get the vehicles and the cameras set up.

She curled up on the van's back seat and closed her eyes. There were advantages to being female, she thought. They were so short of bodies that Joe even had Gareth out there helping to unload equipment. She knew because she could hear him cursing.

The van door opened and Joe said, 'Did you have a rough night, Jill?'

She didn't open her eyes. 'You know I never sleep well the first night I'm in a strange bed.'

'Oh, is that all it was?'

She sat up. 'If you're referring to the portion of the evening that I spent with Scott Richards——'

'I am.'

'Then you obviously know that he went home and I went to my room. Ask the desk clerk if you don't believe me.'

'How did the two of you hit it off?'

'Mind your own business, Joe.'

'What I'm interested in is that you mind yours. And

paying a little attention to the agency's business wouldn't hurt a bit, either, Jill. We are dependent on the town's good will, and anything you could do to leave a good impression would help.'

She sank back into a foetal position. 'Believe me, it was not my idea to be assaulted in the lobby.' She wasn't looking at him, and she missed the startled look in his eyes.

'Assaulted? No, don't tell me. I don't think I want to know. Scott's the president of the Chamber of Commerce, Jill.'

'I know, he's a pillar of the community. I'll be very careful from now on,' she assured Joe, without opening her eyes.

Voices were raised outside the van, and the door opened. 'We don't have a chamois, Joe,' the head cameraman said. 'Walter, that idiot, forgot to bring the——'

'It wasn't on the list, Danny,' the other man said defensively.

Joe sighed. 'Stop arguing about it and somebody go back to town to get one,' he ordered.

'I'll go,' Gareth offered cheerfully.

'No, you can be helping to set the machines up. Jill, do you drive?'

Jill opened one eye. 'Yes, Joe. I haven't always lived in Manhattan. But——'

'Then you can go. And step on it; we'll be waiting. Anything else you need besides a chamois, guys?'

'A fifth of Scotch might come in handy before the morning is out,' the assistant cameraman muttered. He flipped the van keys at Jill.

'Just one problem,' said Jill. 'What's a chamois?'

'Haven't you ever washed a car, Donovan?'

She nodded. 'I used to take my mother's station

wagon through the automatic carwash when I was a kid.'

There were groans. 'Get some sponges, too, and a bucket. The dust is about a mile thick on those bikes from the gravel road. Why you couldn't find a place on a paved highway, Joe——'

Jill looked out at the confusion at the edge of the field and decided it would be easier to do as she was told. She settled herself in the driver's seat and looked warily over the controls. She had never handled anything quite this large before; driving her parents' little car around Baltimore when she went to visit them didn't compare. But then, she told herself firmly, one never forgot how, either, and a van wasn't really any different from a passenger car. It wasn't as if they had put her behind the wheel of a ten-ton truck.

'This isn't a practical joke, is it, Joe?' she muttered. 'The guys wouldn't send me all the way into town for something that doesn't exist, just for the fun of laughing at me when I come back without it, would they?'

'Not this time. I arranged for a charge account at the hardware store, by the way, just for this sort of occasion.'

'That figures,' Jill muttered. 'That's just exactly where I wanted to go this morning.'

She drove slowly, wary of the shifting gravel surface, and she was almost into town before her confidence returned. Then she wished it hadn't, because it gave her a chance to think about Scott and what had happened last night. She had assumed that, once his point had been made, Scott wouldn't come within a mile of her, and she had decided to stay a good way from him, as well. Not that she was afraid of what might happen, exactly, she told herself. But she was here to do a job, and that was the only thing of importance right now—getting those darned pictures taken so that she could leave Springhill behind for ever.

But instead of minding her own business, here she was sticking her head inside the lion's den again.

Don't be foolish, she told herself. You sound as if you expect him to be waiting on the front step to sweep you off your feet with another kiss. Maybe I'll be lucky, and he won't even be at work yet.

Joe had pointed out the hardware store as they had left town that morning. It had been another revelation for Jill, who had pictured a narrow old brick building on the town square, with high tin ceilings and dim lights and a basement crammed with bins and barrels that had been there for a hundred years. 'And probably,' she jeered at herself, 'the proprietor wearing a canvas apron as he weighs out nails—you've been watching too many old movies, Jill Donovan.'

Instead, Springhill Hardware was a sprawling structure on the edge of town, part of a strip of new shops. She parked the van in the far corner of the lot, where she had plenty of manoeuvring room. Whoever heard of a hardware store in a shopping mall? she asked herself. Malls were the habitat of clothing boutiques and shoe stores and shops crammed with linens and candles and crystal, not hammers and bolts and wires.

She crossed the threshold and pulled up short in front of a display of lawnmowers and window air-conditioners. But it was the glass case of gorgeously cut crystal in the next aisle that had grabbed her attention. 'Well, what next?' she muttered.

'May I help you, ma'am?'

Jill's green eyes went wide with embarrassment at being caught talking to herself. At her elbow was a very young man who wore a dark blue shirt with a monogram on the pocket. 'Do you work here?' she asked, then chided herself on the idiocy of the question. How many ordinary citizens would be walking around Springhill wearing a shirt like that?

'Yes, ma'am.' Her dark-fringed eyes had the same effect on him as they did on most males, she noticed with regret; the young man's voice cracked into an adolescent squeal. He swallowed hard and said, 'Are you interested in a lawnmower?'

'No,' she said regretfully. 'Just a chamois.'

To her relief, he didn't look at her in bewilderment. She still half-believed that the guys in the camera crew had sent her on a wild-goose chase. He led the way down a long, wide, well-lit aisle instead. She scarcely noticed the store, however; she was keeping an eye out for the boss.

That's silly, she told herself. You can't go around all week dodging shadows because of what happened last night. In the first place, you'll only make yourself look guilty. And if you're really feeling rotten about your part in it, which you are, then you should be adult enough to apologise the next time you see Scott, and then you can stop worrying about it altogether. And if you're truly grown-up, you'll tell Cassie you're sorry, too.

No, she decided. I'm not quite that mature.

'She looked in disbelief at the package the young man handed her. 'Leather?' she said. 'They want me to bring back some poor animal's skin to polish the paint on their precious dirt bikes?'

'That's what it's for,' he said, with a shrug.

'I suppose they have a reason, but it seems a bit

cruel to me. Thank you.' Jill gave the young man a dismissing smile.

He swallowed hard, and said hopefully, 'Will there be anything else? Anything else at all?'

She shook her head. Then she saw the expression in his eyes change, and so she wasn't surprised at all when Scott spoke beside her. The young clerk scurried off towards the front of the store to carry out the order he had been given.

Scott leaned against the end of a counter. 'I thought you'd be working this morning.'

'I am. I'm just picking up supplies.'

His eyes drifted down over the length of her body, and Jill was suddenly and painfully aware of just how brief her white shorts were, and how little her dark green T-shirt left to the imagination. She could feel a wave of pink rise in her cheeks, and she wanted to kick herself. She had been surrounded by men all morning, and she hadn't felt this way, because there was really nothing to be embarrassed about; she was adequately covered. Not even the admiration in the young clerk's eyes had bothered her. But let Scott Richards take a second look and she was ready to melt.

It's your own guilty conscience, she told herself.

There were fine lines around his eyes this morning, she realised, as if he hadn't slept any better than she had. He must be regretting, as much as she was, how far things had got out of hand last night, even before that kiss. And perhaps, she thought with regret, he was afraid that she wasn't going to drop it there, that she would insist on retaliating and making a public fuss of it that would rock the whole town. Well, at least she could put his mind to rest about that.

An apology. You make it sound as if you were to blame for it all, she told herself irritably, when he's the one who created the scene with the kiss! But if an apology from her would end this ridiculous tension, it was worth it.

'I'm really sorry about what happened last night,' she began.

At the same instant, he said, 'I want to apologise for my behaviour——'

They both stopped politely, waiting for the other to continue, and in the sudden silence Jill began to giggle uncontrollably. She sat down on the bottom shelf, her long legs folded up, laughing. 'What a pair of idiots we are,' she said finally, and wiped tears of laughter away with a fingertip. 'Both of us were stunned, and we were absolutely terrified that the other was going to rake things up that are long dead. And so that's precisely what we did. Oh, Scott, how utterly silly we must have sounded last night!'

For an instant, he looked at her as if she had gone completely mad, and then he started to laugh as well. 'It was pretty incredible,' he agreed, and reached a hand down to her.

Jill came gracefully to her feet beside him, still giggling. 'I'm so glad things are back to normal,' she said with the easy confidence of a child. 'We are old friends, aren't we, Scott? We just let things get out of hand that autumn, when we thought we were in love, and when that didn't work out, we forgot that we could still be friends.' She looked up at him. The fine lines at his temples had crinkled even more as he laughed, and there were gold flecks of humour in his eyes. She had forgotten how absolutely gorgeous he was when he smiled, and for an instant she felt oddly breathless.

He was still holding her hand, as if he had forgotten it. 'Old friends,' he repeated thoughtfully. 'You're right. Jill. Perhaps we should start all over again, as if you had just got into town.'

She nodded cheerfully, and said, with a teasing sparkle, 'It's awfully nice to see you again, Scott.'

'Likewise. Why don't you come and have dinner with us tonight, so we can catch up on old times?'

It felt like a punch in the stomach. Go to his home, and face Cassie, who would certainly, by now, have stopped being trusting and naïve? Get yourself out of this one, Donovan, she ordered. I didn't exactly mean that we should be pals——

She looked down at her slender fingers, still lying in his hand, and discarded one excuse after another. They wouldn't be working late; the light would be wrong, and besides, Joe had made that appointment with the women's editor at the newspaper. She obviously didn't have another engagement, and a week in the crew's company would be plenty; she didn't think Scott would believe that she was dying to have dinner with them tonight. In fact, she couldn't see a single loophole. She could just say she didn't want to come, of course, but that was hardly a friendly attitude. And she would run into Cassie some time; she might as well get it over with.

She bit her lip. What if he hadn't meant it sincerely, and was expecting her to have an excuse?

Then that's his problem, she decided, and said, before her nerve had a chance to vanish completely, 'I'd like that.'

Her acceptance didn't seem to bother him, but neither, she noticed, did he appear particularly ecstatic. 'Eight o'clock. I'll pick you up if you like, but the house is only three blocks from your motel.'

Jill shook her head. 'I'll get myself there. Just tell me which direction.'

A small child, perhaps five years old, skidded around the corner from the next aisle and crashed into Scott, who caught him and set him back on his feet. 'Can I go for ice cream?' he demanded. 'Bobby's mother says I can if it's all right with you. Please, Daddy?'

Daddy. So there wasn't only a little girl just past babyhood in the Richards house, Jill thought, but a small tornado of a boy as well.

It's a good thing you came to your senses, Jill, she thought. How foolish of you actually to believe that he wanted to turn the clock back and have an affair with you once more. He would never risk his family. He had always wanted a little boy . . .

'Much as I hate to claim him sometimes,' Scott told her with an air of long-suffering patience, 'this is my son. Josh, please dust off your manners long enough to say hello to Miss Donovan. She's having dinner with us tonight.'

The child sent a surprised look up at her through long lashes that looked impossibly dark against his freckled cheeks. He stuck out a hand, and only then did Jill realise that hers was still firmly in Scott's grasp. She freed it gently and willed herself to act as if it were the most normal thing in the world for the child to see her holding hands with his father.

He doesn't look much like Scott, she thought. His hair was too fair, so blond that it was almost white, and his face was a narrow triangle that looked almost too small for his big brown eyes. The eyes were Scott's, she thought. The rest must be Cassie.

His duty done, Josh turned back to his father. 'Can I, Daddy?' he asked again. 'She's waiting for me in the car.'

Scott nodded, and the child was off, the soles of his

running shoes squeaking against the tile floor. Jill's eyes followed him till he was out of sight. 'He's a very attractive child, Scott,' she said.

'He's a good boy.' Quietly, he said, 'Do you regret not having a family, Jill?'

'Me?' It was quick, almost shrill. 'Of course not. I never did think that I was right for the part, remember?' Then she wanted to bite her tongue off. Once, she had thought of having children, his children. The idea had frightened her to death, and yet . . .

He seemed to look straight through her, and then he smiled, a social gesture, cool and meaningless, from a businessman to a customer. 'Is there anything else you need today?'

Jill looked around quickly and found the chamois on the floor at her feet. 'No, just this.' She bent to pick it up and realised that she was a bit breathless. Time for some exercise, Donovan, she told herself. You're getting badly out of shape. 'I'll see you tonight then.'

'Tonight?' It was abstracted, as if he had forgotten. 'Of course. It'll be casual, we'll grill steaks or something.'

She wished she hadn't reminded him of it. He sounded as if he would have liked to forget the whole idea.

The crew gave her no mercy when they discovered that she had forgotten the sponges and the bucket. 'So next time make me a list,' she retorted crossly.

'I'll bet you didn't forget to flirt with your friend the hardware person,' jibed Gareth.

Joe Niemann followed her into the back of the van. 'What's eating you, Donovan?'

'Isn't Gareth's heavy-handed humour enough?' Jill snapped open a make-up case, and inspected her nose in the mirror. 'Why did you decide to shoot this campaign here, anyway?' she demanded.

He shrugged. 'It's not as easy as it sounds to find a place, you know. Not every farmer is anxious to let us knock down a whole field of corn to shoot a set of ads, even if he's well paid for his trouble.'

'I didn't mean this specific farm, though heaven knows it's certainly far enough from civilisation. I meant, why Springhill, Joe? Did you play pin-the-tail-on-the-donkey with a map of the Midwest, or what?'

'Something tells me you had another run-in with Scott Richards. Donovan, why in the world can't you——'

'The guys are yelling for you,' she pointed out crisply. 'And I'm going to change clothes so I'm ready to shoot. Do you mind giving me a little privacy, Joe?' She shut the curtains on the van windows with an emphatic snap, and he retreated.

They tried all morning, without much success. The tall stalks of corn didn't want to co-operate; instead of lying down in a neat row as the all-terrain vehicles passed slowly over them, they went every which way. One slapped Jill across the nose so hard that she expected to have a red welt there for days.

And, with every attempt, several rows of corn stalks lay broken on the ground, and they had to move the cameras, polish the machines, and start all over again.

After the third try, Joe Niemann stood in the middle of the field for a long while, frowning and pulling at his lower lip. Then he announced, 'We're going to have to speed up. If the bikes move a little faster, the effect will be better.'

'These things are dangerous, you know,' Jill complained as her vehicle jolted across a small ridge

in the field. She was scared to death of the thing; she
had never been much of a fan of motorised toys.

'What a chicken you are,' said Gareth as his
machine roared up next to hers. 'I'd like to take mine
out on the road and see what it can do.' He revved the
engine.

So maybe he's not as protective of his own skin as I
thought, Jill decided. But he's crazy if he does it. That
machine is unstable.

'This is not the Grand Prix, Gareth,' Joe told him.
'I said a little faster, not racing speed.'

Jill put her wide-brimmed straw hat on to protect
her nose from the sun while the cameras were moved.
It was the part of her job that she liked least—the
constant waiting. She had long ago learned to retreat
into her own thoughts, with just enough of her
attention on the job to alert her when it was time to go
back to work. But today, her thoughts were not the
most inviting place to be. She seemed unable to escape
from the past.

*'I never did think that I was right for the part,
remember?'* What a way to begin, if she wanted to put
the past behind them . . .

It had been a cold night in early December, and it
had been snowing a little, when Scott had asked her to
marry him. He had been pacing the floor of the little
sitting-room at the sorority house when she came
down, and the strain and tension in his face had
frightened her. He had told her about his father's
sudden illness, and that he was leaving right then, as
soon as he had broken the news to her, to go home.

'But I couldn't go without saying goodbye to you,'
he had said. 'It's very bad, and if he doesn't make
it——' His voice had broken, then, and she had put her
arms around him in silent comfort while he tried to

deal with the unbearable. 'In any case, he won't be able to go back to work for a while, so I'll have to stay and run the store.'

Jill hadn't understood that at all. 'And sacrifice the whole semester's work? You can't do that, Scott.'

'I have to. It's Christmas season, and someone has to take charge. If I'm there, Jill, then Dad can relax and get well. If I'm not, well, he'll be fretting about the store.'

She hadn't argued about it; it made no sense at all to her, but obviously he was convinced that it was the only way. 'Do what you have to,' she had said finally. 'You can come back next semester.'

'But that's just it, you see. I don't know when I'll be back, or even if I'll be able to leave at all. It will be months before he's well enough to go back to work.' He took a deep breath, and said, 'Perhaps it really doesn't matter. I'm just going back a little earlier than I'd planned.'

Jill had stared at him in bewilderment. 'What do you mean, a little earlier? You'll graduate in the spring.' Realisation dawned in her eyes. 'Do you mean to intend to go back there to spend your life, Scott Richards?'

'Of course,' he said flatly, as if there had never been any doubt. 'It's my home.' He seized her hands. 'Jill, I want you to come with me. Not today, of course, there's no sense in both of us throwing the semester away. But you'll come at Christams, won't you, as soon as finals are over? And you'll stay?'

'Stay?' The single word held in it all the incredulity she felt. 'You mean, come there to live? For ever?'

'There's really no reason for us to wait. I need you with me, I need your support. And it's not as if an art history degree will do you much good in a small town, anyway.'

'You're damned right it wouldn't' Jill said tartly. 'What happened to New York, and the big advertising agency on Madison Avenue where you were going to get a job?'

'Oh, it's fun to dream. But I've always known that I was going home some day.'

Jill pulled her hands out of his. 'Well, I wish you'd shared that insight with me a little earlier,' she snapped. 'It could have saved us both a lot of trouble.'

Scott looked stunned. 'Jill, I'm asking you to marry me,' he pointed out.

'And I'm telling you that you can do as you like, but there is a world out there, Scott, and I'm not going to turn my back on it.' It isn't fair, her heart was screaming. 'You lied to me, Scott,' she accused. 'I've never made any secret of what I expected.'

'No,' he said slowly, 'you haven't. But I thought——'

'You thought that as soon as you announced that I'd won you in the marriage lottery, I'd give up everything I've ever wanted in order to claim my prize, is that it? My God, Scott, I had no idea what a chauvinist you were! Isn't what I want important too?'

'Is it so very different, Jill? I want to marry you. I want to have children with you, and raise them to be good human beings——'

'In some stupid little town in Iowa? Is that what you think I want out of life, to be stuck in the middle of nowhere warming up bottles? Men have careers and women have children, is that what you mean? Well, think about it again, Scott. Not this woman. I don't plan to be tied down with babies; I'm not right for the part.'

His face had gone white. 'I know there wouldn't be as many opportunities for you in a small town,' he began.

'I'll bet you can't name a single one.'

'But you love me, Jill. Isn't that important to you.'

'I thought I loved you,' she corrected stiffly. 'Now I see that I don't know you well enough to love you.'

'You care enough about me to go to bed with me,' he pointed out.

I do care about you, she thought, miserably. At least, I cared about the person I thought you were. But you misled me, you hid behind a mask and made me think you were something you weren't. She said, with harsh clarity, 'That is an entirely different thing.'

There was a long silence. 'I see,' he said, and the anger and frustration had died out of his voice, leaving only a tired huskiness behind. 'Perhaps I don't know you as well as I thought, either.' He hadn't bothered to zip his parka or to put on his stocking cap. He had just turned on his heel and gone out into the snow, and she had not seen him again.

The following spring, she had been discovered in an art class by the woman who ran the New York modelling agency she worked for, and she, too, had left the campus without her degree to follow a dream. She had never regretted it for a moment.

I wonder if Scott is sorry sometimes that he came here, she thought. I wonder if he ever went back and finished that final year. Perhaps he had; perhaps that was when he and Cassie had met again . . .

'Donovan!' Joe Niemann sounded furious. 'If you miss another cue, I'm going to send you back to New York!'

Please do, she thought. Perhaps I can get out of town this afternoon. She sighed. That certainly wouldn't solve anything. 'Sorry, Joe.'

The cue was given again, the pair of all-terrain vehicles moved towards the camera in perfect tandem. Just then, a heavy truck sped by on the road, and a cloud of gravel dust rolled across the field, putting a neat coating of grey on the entire scene. Jill choked on the chalky taste of the stuff; Gareth spat and swore. The cameraman groaned and started the difficult process of cleaning the gritty substance off his lenses without scratching the delicate coating on the glass.

Joe Niemann looked up at the sky as if half expecting to be hit by lightning, too. 'That's all for today, guys,' he said disgustedly. 'It's getting too late, and the shadows aren't right for the effect I want. We'll try again tomorrow.'

It was some relief. And of course, as a professional. Jill knew how rarely the first try brought results. 'But it never hurts to hope,' she muttered. 'It can't be too soon for me.'

Joe Niemann was waiting for her in a small meeting-room that he had commandeered for the interview, but the reporter hadn't turned up yet. 'Do you want me to stay?' he asked over the top of his newspaper when Jill came in.

'Please.' She pulled a chair around.

'You look as if you'd been crying. Your eyes are all red.'

'Well, I haven't been sobbing into my pillow,' Jill said tartly. 'The pool must have ten times the recommended level of chlorine in it.'

'Oh, is that all that's bothering you?'

'Isn't that enough?' She inspected herself in a mirrored door. Joe was right; she did look as if she had just indulged in a fit of hysterics. I'll remember that next time I need to conceal tears, she thought. Go jump into the pool and no one will be able to tell.

'The motel manager told me they're having trouble with the filtration system.' He folded the paper, put it aside, and lit a fresh cigar. 'I thought perhaps something else was eating at you. The boys want to try a little restaurant out on the edge of town for dinner. Is that all right with you?'

She willed herself not to turn odd colours. 'I've made other plans,' she said casually.

'Scott Richards.' It was not a question.

'Yes.' I don't owe Joe an explanation, Jill thought. But she found herself awkwardly attempting one anyway. 'We're just going to catch up on old news, Joe. I haven't seen him in years.'

He didn't comment, but Jill thought he looked sceptical. 'I guess I jumped to the wrong conclusion about your run-in with him last night. I hadn't heard about the lobby extravaganza then, you see. I thought you'd had a fight.'

Jill tried to hide her sigh. 'There was nothing to it.'

'Well, watch out for him. And don't cause trouble for me.'

She said, 'Let me make one thing very clear, Joe. Despite what the desk clerk thinks he saw last night, I don't mess around with married men.' Her voice was sharp.

'Scott Richards isn't married.'

'Really?' she asked sarcastically. 'Then what do you call that thing he wears on his left hand? A charm bracelet?'

'Oh, it's a wedding ring all right. He never took it off after his wife died.'

'Died?' It was a hoarse whisper; Jill's throat felt

raw, as if she had screamed the word.

'They say he hasn't looked at another woman since. I wouldn't know, myself, but I'd say they're wrong, considering your experience last night and all.' Joe puffed the cigar into glowing life; the smoke formed a sort of halo around his head. He didn't look at her.

But there's Cassie, she thought, and the baby, and his little boy. Joe has to be wrong, she told herself desperately. It was someone else they were talking about, not Scott. It couldn't have been Scott . . .

CHAPTER FOUR

THE reporter arrived just then, and there was no time to think. Jill went through the interview in a sort of daze, not knowing at the end quite what she had said, but glad that Joe Niemann was there; she was certain that she had sounded reasonably professional, or Joe would have stepped in and prevented her from making a fool of herself.

'Are you sure you don't want to have dinner with the crew?' Joe asked after the interview was over.

I'd love to, Jill thought, but she shook her head. She had accepted an invitation, and running away from it wasn't going to solve anything. Joe looked as if he was going to ask questions, so she said quickly, 'I think I'll go for a walk.'

She stopped in her room just long enough to pick up her camera, she had no real intention of taking pictures, but it would make a good excuse for wandering around Springhill, and to change her high-heeled shoes for more comfortable ones. Scott had said it would be a casual evening.

Scott. Was Joe right? Joe Niemann wasn't known for making embarrassing mistakes, that was certain. But how could Jill herself have been so badly mistaken? She had been so certain, from what Cassie had said. But just what had Cassie said last night at the party?

The effort of remembering brought an abstracted frown to her face, and she was surprised when a woman she met on the pavement paused and then said, kindly, 'Is there a problem, miss?'

Jill blinked. 'Oh, no—thank you.'

The woman smiled. 'You're new to town, aren't you? Welcome!'

'Small town,' Jill muttered to herself as she walked on. 'Everyone minds everyone else's business.' And yet, she reflected, the woman hadn't sounded nosey. She had seemed to be honestly concerned.

She reached the edge of the river and turned away from the street to wander down the bank to the edge of the water. The lowering sun sent shafts of golden light reflecting off the arches of the bridge downstream, framing a man in waders who stood motionless in the shallow water, holding a fishing-rod.

Jill moved quietly around him. She took half a dozen pictures before she was satisfied that she had captured the light and the mood on film. It soothed her; it always did to have a camera in her hands.

Finished, she sat down on a rock. A mallard floated lazily in the almost-still water at the river's edge, and she watched him thoughtfully through her telephoto lens until he turned, as co-operative as any professional model, to give her precisely the angle she wanted. A bullfrog uttered a deep, throaty cry from the edge of a marshy area just a few feet from her. She captured him on film, too, without stirring from her rock, thinking about how even in the middle of town the countryside surrounded her.

It was so quiet here, with the lazy water and the ducks and the frog, with no one asking questions, no one intruding on her thoughts. Springhill might be boring, Jill told herself, but it was certainly peaceful. She wanted to sit on this rock for ever. Certainly she didn't want to walk up to Scott Richards' front door tonight and ring the bell, and spend the evening making charming conversation——

And why not? she asked herself harshly. If she really believed what she had said to him this morning in the hardware store, then spending the evening with him should be no strain at all. It certainly didn't matter to her whether Scott was married or not. All those years ago, they had made the mistake of thinking, for a few brief weeks, that they might spend their lives together. That had not been possible, but they could still be friends.

Not the best-buddies kind of friends, Jill thought, with a sort of shiver, but the kind that exchanged Christmas cards, at least. The kind that went out to lunch, whenever they found themselves in the same town, and swapped stories about their lives.

It made her feel sad, and at the same time, almost relieved. Their break-up had been a loose end left dangling for too long, a door that had never been firmly shut, but that had no chance of ever being opened again, either. Now they had another chance to finish it, to heal the wounds——

What wounds? she asked herself harshly. You're sounding like a sentimental fool, Jill Donovan. What Joe told me tonight, whether it was true or not, didn't change anything. Obviously Scott had dealt with his wounds long ago, before he married whatever-her-name-was. And you—well, you got rid of your hurts a long time ago, too. You had scarcely thought about him for years, until you came here. And why you didn't have the sense this morning to say, 'Gee, I'm glad to know that you're doing all right, Scott, but it was a long time ago, and let's not bother to catch up on all the years in between.'

Well, she hadn't said it. She had agreed to come to dinner instead. And it was too late to do anything about it now. So she picked up her expensive foreign camera and the two extra lenses and started walking, following the directions he had given her.

Clearview Court was badly named, she decided the instant she turned off the main street and into the little cul-de-sac. There wasn't a clear view of anything from here, just large modern homes set far apart on green lawns, surrounded by huge old trees. Near the entrance to the court, a new house was going up. It was quiet at this hour, with all the workers gone—just a skeleton standing tall against the darkening sky, surrounded by irregular piles of dirt and a litter of supply scraps. The scent of freshly made sawdust still hovered, accompanied by the gentle smell of newly mown grass from down the block.

At the end of the court the dead-end street widened into a traffic circle where several small children were riding bicycles. It was a neighbourhood for children, and Jill thought it was unusual that there were so few in sight. But perhaps it was bath and bedtime, she thought. How little she knew about children!

For the first time in her life, she felt just a little pinch of regret about that, and it startled her. For many women, she knew, having a child was the most important thing in life. Jill had never felt that way; what she had said to Scott that morning at the hardware store was true. She didn't think she was the naturally maternal sort. She had never spent much time worrying about it, however. No matter how she had felt about it, the fact was that the life of a model didn't allow for the flexibility required to have a family. The girl who took a few months off to have a baby ran the risk that she would be forgotten, her niche filled by another pretty face, by the time she was ready to return.

And Jill's career was far too important to her to take that sort of risk. Some day, perhaps, she would change her mind, she thought, especially if this tiny twinge of regret was any indication. When she found a man she could spend her life with, well, then she would worry about whether she could ever become a decent parent. But there had never been a man. Or at least, she told herself, she had never found the right man, the man who understood the importance of her career, and who didn't expect her to stay at home and strain baby food instead.

Goodness, she thought with wry humour, recognising how very far her thoughts had strayed. I've only been in this little town for two days, and my mind has already started to soften!

Scott's house was at the very end of the court, a contemporary design sided with cedar that had weathered to a pleasant silvery grey. It didn't look like a large house, nestled as it was into the side of a gentle hill that sloped down away from the street towards a wooded ravine. Behind the house, a high cedar fence closed the lawn off from the rest of the neighbourhood. It was a visible reminder, Jill realised, of what a private person Scott really was, underneath the surface charm.

She took a deep breath and pushed the doorbell. What would the house be like inside? she wondered. Would it be a shrine to his lost love? Might that be why he had invited her here—to show her how little she had mattered, after all?

She heard the bell, sounding a muted melody behind the double front doors. But there was no answering pattern of footsteps. No sound at all, she reflected. She stood uncertainly on the step for a moment, tried the bell again, gave up. Irritation

began to nag at her, and fear that she had been made
to look foolish.

Just as she gave up and started across the lawn to
the road again, she heard a squeak from the side of the
house, and turned to see Cassie coming through a gate
in the cedar fence, with a small child on her hip.

Cassie waved and hurried across the grass to her.
'Did you ring the bell? Scott's around the back, on the
patio. I don't think he can hear it from there.'

'Careless of him,' Jill murmured. 'He almost missed
out on having a guest.' She wasn't quite sure if she
should be relieved at Cassie's presence; the only thing
she knew for certain was that she was confused. Cassie
didn't sound much like a hostess greeting a guest, and
yet here she was. Had Joe's st ry been simply the
result of a misunderstanding?

'I'll take you around,' Cassie said, and started back
across the lawn. 'Speaking of guests, I'm having a
party tomorrow to celebrate Jamie's birthday. I'd like
to have you come. Sort of a picnic in my back yard—I
live next door.' She waved a casual hand at a split-
level house painted rusty brown.

Well, Jill thought with a sigh of relief, that seems to
settle that. She was glad to know, finally; it would
have been a little embarrassing if she had ended up
asking Scott, or even Cassie herself, for the truth. It
would have made the whole thing sound too
important, somehow.

'Six o'clock,' Cassie went on, and reached for the
latch on the gate. 'Come early if you can and we'll
have a glass of tea and a good gossip before the crowd
gathers.' She raised her voice. 'Look who I found on
your front step, Scott. I told you that doorbell isn't
loud enough.'

For a moment, Jill didn't see him. Then she realised

why the back garden had been fenced; a great deal of it was occupied by a large swimming-pool, and all that was visible of Scott at the moment was a wet head in the water. He struck out for the side with a powerful stroke, and as he pulled himself from the pool, Jill sucked in a silent and admiring breath. He was wearing a red swimsuit so brief that it was barely decent, and every muscle in his body was tautly outlined under the wet brown skin.

She stole a glance at Cassie, wanting to see how this display affected her. But Cassie was watching Jill instead, with a set, almost shocked, look in her eyes.

Jill released the breath she had been holding, trying to seem casual about it. What had happened, anyway? she asked herself in confusion. Cassie had been perfectly friendly, even charming, until that moment. What had happened so suddenly to change the congenial look in her eyes to hostility? All I did was look at him, Jill thought. No woman could have ignored that display, or found it unattractive. It certainly was nothing for Cassie to be jealous of.

Jealousy? Had that been it? Jill turned it over in her mind. Did Cassie have her eye on Scott? The theory answered all the requirements, Jill decided, and wondered once more what had brought Cassie to Springhill. If it hadn't been Scott, as she had originally believed—but perhaps it had been, she thought.

Well, if she's trying to warn me off her territory, Jill thought, she needn't bother. Of course I found him physically attractive. Any woman with eyes would have. But that's a long way from wanting anything more.

Scott picked up a towel from the edge of the pool and came towards them, rubbing his hair. 'Sorry I didn't hear you, Jill,' he said. 'I didn't realise how late it was. Thanks, Cassie.'

Cassie smiled, but the strain hadn't gone out of her eyes. 'And goodnight,' she added. 'Don't worry, Scott, I can take a hint.' The child in her arms made a fussy little murmur and Cassie dropped a kiss on her brow. 'Sleepy, Jamie? I should think so, after the day you've had.' Her voice was gentle as she smoothed the child's hair. 'I'll be expecting Josh as usual in the morning.' She didn't wait for an answer.

Scott draped his towel over the back of a chair on the cedar deck and put on a short terry-cloth robe. He didn't bother to tie the belt, but at least the majority of him was covered now. Jill found it a lot more comfortable.

'I wonder what's bothering Cassie,' she said casually.

Scott looked across the lawn after the woman with a tiny frown between his eyes. 'I didn't notice,' he said finally. 'Just tired, I expect. It's hard work to chase a year-old baby all day.'

And that, Jill thought, shows how observant he is! 'Surely she doesn't have to do it all alone,' she said. 'I mean, her husband must help.'

Scott shook his head. 'He walked out on her not long after Jamie was born. He announced one day that fatherhood was not his idea of fun, and left.'

It gave her a sinking sort of emptiness in the pit of her stomach. 'Charming of him,' Jill said curtly.

He looked up from the charcoal grill with surprise. 'I thought you'd be applauding his courage at doing what was important to him, regardless of the consequences. After all, you agree with him, don't you?' He reached for a plate that held two magnificent T-bone steaks and a hot dog, and plopped them on to a rack above the glowing coals.

'Oh, for heaven's sake, Scott, don't twist my words. I don't have anything against kids, I've just chosen not to have any myself. That's a little different from abandoning an infant, you know.' She drew herself up straight. 'Perhaps you'd rather I just went back to the motel now.'

'And waste a perfectly good steak? Of course not.' He wasn't looking at her; he was watching the shallow end of the pool, where a little boy was splashing wildly. 'Sorry, Jill. I shouldn't have compared you to Cassie's husband.' He grinned at her, suddenly. 'You're much prettier, for one thing.'

'Thanks.' It was stiff. 'You're still the complete chauvinist, aren't you?'

'Now how can you accuse me of that, when I'm the one who's cooking?' he said mildly. 'Do you still like your steaks rare?'

She nodded, vaguely surprised that he had remembered.

'There's Perrier for you in the cooler on the picnic table, by the way. Beer, too, if you'd rather have that.'

Jill twisted the cap off the Perrier and took a long drink straight from the bottle. Her walk had left her warm and sticky, and the cold liquid felt wonderful. She would have liked to pour it over her head. 'You're lucky to have a pool,' she said wistfully.

'Didn't I tell you to bring a suit? Sorry, that must have been the moment Josh arrived at the store this morning. I think there's one around somewhere.'

Cassie's? she wondered. Or his wife's? She shook her head. 'I had a swim at the motel. It was a little crowded, though. Can I help with the food?' The cooler was full of containers nested in ice, macaroni salad in one bowl, she saw, and something that looked like green beans in another. 'You weren't kidding about cooking, were you?'

'Oh, that?' He shook his head. 'Most of it came from the supermarket deli, I'm afraid. If life was fair, they'd have made me a shareholder by now, I've spent so much money there. Would you get me a beer?'

She popped the top of the can open and handed it to him, then sat down on the end of the bench with her knees drawn up and her arms folded around them, the Perrier bottle dangling between two fingers. 'How long have you and Josh been on your own?' she asked.

He didn't look at her as he carefully turned the steaks. 'A little more than four years.'

She was shocked. 'But Josh is——'

'He's six. He'll start first grade in the fall.'

Jill looked out at the youngster in the pool, wondering if he had even a vague memory of his mother. Did children remember things that happened before they were two? Six years old, she mused. Her estimate of his age, that morning, had been close. Well, it confirmed her suspicion that it hadn't taken long for Scott to get over her and marry—what *was* her name?

And if he could forget me so easily, she thought, I should be thankful that I didn't marry him. And I am.

'How do you manage?' she asked, curiously. 'I can't imagine——'

Scott shrugged. 'Cassie takes care of him during the day. The money helps her out, too, so she can stay at home with the baby. He's going to spend a couple of weeks later in the summer with my mother to give me a break, and——'

'Your mother? Then——' She stopped, abruptly.

'My father died last winter.'

There was a long silence. 'I'm sorry, Scott.'

He nodded shortly, as if he resented having to accept her concern. 'How are your parents?' he asked, finally.

He had met them just once that autumn, she remembered, when they had come from Baltimore for parents' weekend at the university. His parents hadn't come. There had been something special going on at the store, and they couldn't leave. No wonder his father had had that heart attack, she thought idly. He had never learned to relax.

She realised abruptly that she hadn't answered his question. 'They're fine,' she said. 'Dad retired a couple of years ago, and they do a lot more travelling now. In fact, they're in France at the moment. Sunning themselves on the Riviera, if I've got the timetable straight.' And you're babbling, Jill, she told herself sternly.

'I wish my father had done something like that,' he murmured. 'It was only last year that he agreed to move to Arizona. And then he didn't have much time to enjoy it.'

But his death leaves you free, she thought. Haven't you thought of that, Scott? You could go anywhere you liked, now, you could pick up your career—— Then she was heartily ashamed of herself for even thinking it. Freedom, if it came at the cost of his father's life, was nothing Scott would be pleased with.

'Mother likes it down there, though. She's going to stay. 'Josh!' Scott called. 'Time to get out of the water!'

Two small hands clutched the edge of the pool, and a water-darkened head shook decisively. 'I don't want to,' Josh announced.

'Too bad. Your hot dog is ready.'

'I don't want to eat. I'm not hungry.' It was positive.

'You know the rule. If you don't get out the first time you're told, there'll be no swimming tomorrow. You have sixty seconds.' Scott didn't sound concerned about it. He turned his back on the child and started to take containers out of the cooler.

Jill sat very still and watched the child from the corner of her eye; he was obviously struggling with his decision. Scott seemed to be paying no attention at all. It took nearly the full minute before the rebellion in the pool collapsed. Then Josh climbed out of the water and trailed across the patio, leaving small wet footprints in an uneven line. He circled Jill warily and stood beside his father, his thumb in his mouth, until his hot dog was on his plate and doused with ketchup.

'In case you're feeling sorry for him,' Scott said drily as he took Jill's steak off the grill, 'don't. I'm not being cheap. Josh has tried every food in the world and pronounced only hot dogs, peanut butter, and spaghetti fit to eat.'

Jill, who had been thinking it a bit unfair that the child wasn't allowed to have a steak, coloured a little.

'They tell me that children, especially boys, don't appreciate good food until they reach the age when they're hungry all the time,' Scott went on thoughtfully. 'Then they learn to like steak and lobster and, knowing Josh, probably caviare as well.' He handed her the plate. 'It's nice to have someone around who appreciates adult-type food.'

What about Cassie? she almost asked, and bit her lip. It was certainly none of her business. She cut into her steak instead. It was perfect, juicy and red.

'How did the photo session go today?'

Are you anxious to know when we'll be gone? she wondered, and then told herself not to be silly. It was only idle conversation, after all. 'Not particularly

well. It's rare that we get what we're after on the first
try, of course, but usually we have something. Today
was a total loss.'

Scott nodded, as if he wasn't surprised. 'Why
cornfields, anyway? I mean, I'm glad that you're
here——'

It's very nice of him to say that, she thought, with a
little spark of joy in her heart.

'It's good for the town's economy,' he went on, and
the spark went out. 'But it seems an odd way to
advertise an all-terrain vehicle. A snowmobile,
perhaps, running across a field with a few odd
cornstalks that were left after the harvest—that would
make sense, but——'

Jill groaned. 'Please don't tell Joe that,' she begged.
'North Star makes snowmobiles, too.'

Scott's eyes lit up. 'Perhaps they'd let you wear an
ermine jacket,' he said. 'With your hair——' He
reached across the table as if to touch a long, silky
lock.

Jill flipped it back over her shoulder. 'If it's all the
same to you, I'd rather go to the Florida Keys and
model swimsuits. At any rate, if the company isn't
happy with these photos, none of us will have to
worry about the snowmobiles.'

'You're on trial?'

She nodded. 'Not even the ad agency has worked for
North Star before. They fired the last one when sales
dropped. So if Joe Niemann seems to be gruff
sometimes, it's because his job is on the line.'

'What about yours?'

Jill shook her head. 'I'm not under contract to them
or anything. Once Joe has his photos, I'm finished.'

He shook his head. 'I still don't understand why
you're doing this. Modelling is a long way from being

a museum curator.'

'But it pays better. And it's certainly not dull. Next week I'll be shooting for a magazine cover in New York, and the week after that, I have no idea, but it will be different.'

'What are you going to do after your modelling career is over?'

'Why are you so certain it's coming to an end? I'm not ready to apply for a pension yet, Scott.'

He didn't answer. 'You didn't eat your steak,' he said finally. 'Was there something wrong with it?'

She glanced down at her plate. 'Of course not. It was wonderful.'

'You only ate a few bites.'

'Scott, there was more meat on that steak than I usually allow myself in three days.'

'You'd look better if you had a little more flesh on you.'

'Not in front of the cameras, I wouldn't.' She looked at him steadily, and finally forced herself to laugh. 'I'm not anorexic, you know.'

'Just too darned skinny.'

'But that's not your concern.' She gestured at Josh's plate, where his hot dog lay in bits. 'Scott, really. You haven't said a word about that hot-dog.'

He had never been particularly graceful in defeat, she thought. He looked at her for a long time, and a muscle twitched in his cheek. Then without a word he picked up his plate and hers and went into the house.

Josh had long since given up any pretence of eating; he was drawing ketchup lines with his fork. He looked up suddenly and announced, 'I like you. You didn't give me a smothery hug and tell me how cute I am.'

Jill, who had been beginning to think the child had developed laryngitis since she had seen him that morning, was disarmed by the sudden friendliness.

'I have a loose tooth,' he bragged. 'Want to see it?'

This, she thought, must be the pass-key into a little boy's world. 'Of course I'd like to see it.'

The loose tooth was one of his front ones, and it wriggled convincingly when Josh prodded it with a finger. 'Bobby's already lost both his front teeth,' he announced. 'And the tooth fairy brought him two quarters.'

'How lucky for him.'

'Would you help me catch lightning bugs?'

'I think perhaps I'd better help your father clean up the mess here instead.'

Josh scowled. 'I want you to help me!'

'I knew it was too good to last,' said Scott, as he came across the deck with two mugs. 'His silence, I mean.'

'You mean he isn't usually shy?'

'This kid knows more people in town than I do. I don't know what got into him earlier tonight. Coffee, Jill?'

'I don't drink it; the caffeine is bad for my skin.' Then she saw the look on his face.

'Not even one cup of coffee? And no alcohol, I see. I suppose you don't eat sweets, either. What do you do to celebrate, Jill? Chew a stick of sugarless gum?'

'You don't need to be sarcastic, Scott.' She eyed the steaming mug with caution. It did look good. 'I guess one cup can't hurt.' Besides, it was easier to drink it than to argue with him about it. She reached for the mug.

Josh stamped his foot and said, more loudly, 'I want her to catch lightning bugs with me!'

Scott's eyebrows went up. He turned to stare down at his small son as if he couldn't quite believe what he had heard. 'If you wish to continue this tantrum, Josh, feel free to go to your room so that we don't interrupt you,' he said politely.

Josh stared at his own toes, shifting uneasily on the deck, for a long moment. Then he shook his head.

'Then you may go and play for a few minutes.'

Jill watched Josh go off across the lawn and shook her head. 'I've never seen anything like that.'

Scott waved a hand at the cushioned loveseat. 'Josh is a good kid,' he said. 'I'm just determined he's going to stay that way.'

'You seem to have found the method.' She started to put covers back on the containers of food. 'Can I help you take these things back in?'

Scott shook his head. 'I'm just going to shove everything into the refrigerator. Make yourself comfortable.'

She ignored the loveseat. To sit there and wait for him, she thought, might leave the wrong impression. She pulled a lawn chair around so that she could look out over the now still water of the pool. Josh, on the far side of it, was stretching as high as he could to capture a firefly. For an instant, the child's body seemed to form a living sculpture in the dying light. Without an instant's hesitation Jill set her coffee aside, reached for her camera, and went down across the grass towards him.

He turned and smiled at her and held out his trophy, now safely enclosed in a small glass jar, and she pressed the shutter release.

'There was no flash,' Josh complained.

'I don't need one, because I'm using a special kind of film. There's another lightning bug.' He danced away after it, seeming to forget about her, and she followed. It wasn't until the last of her film was used that she realised that the light had rapidly dimmed, and that Scott was standing on the edge of the deck, his arms folded, wearing a frown. He was fully dressed; the terry robe had given way to jeans and running shoes and a polo shirt.

'I don't want to have a bath,' Josh said grumpily. 'The swimming-pool got me clean.'

Jill realised that Scott must have been calling, and that she had been so engrossed that she hadn't heard. She held out a hand to Josh. 'I see what you mean. But I think we'd better to to the house this minute or the pool will be off limits for both of us tomorrow.'

Josh thought that one over and grinned. 'Will you come and swim with me tomorrow?'

You and your big mouth, Donovan, she accused herself. 'I haven't been invited to come back, Josh.'

'Yes, you have,' he pointed out. 'I asked you. Daddy says I can ask my friends to come and play.'

The casual acceptance of her as a friend warmed her heart. It ought to amuse his father too, she thought, considering how Josh had reacted when she first arrived. They climbed the little slope hand in hand, and it wasn't until they reached the edge of the deck that she looked up at Scott.

He was watching her with wary caution. No, she thought, half confused, half frightened, it was more than that. He was looking at her with something in his eyes that looked like hate.

Then he moved and smiled, and Jill released a breath that she hadn't even known she had been holding. It had been just a trick of the failing light which had put that harsh expression on his face. That was all.

She was relieved. Just a few short days and she would be gone, and she would probably never see him again. But she didn't want to leave with unpleasantness between them. She didn't want him to hate her . . .

CHAPTER FIVE

'I DIDN'T hear you call,' she said, trying to keep her voice light. 'Sorry.'

'You were obviously absorbed. Josh, your bath water is getting cold.' Scott watched the child until he was safely inside the house, and dropped into a chair as if he was exhausted.

'Chasing Cassie's baby may be a full-time job, as you said,' Jill observed, 'but it looks to me as if you don't have an easy time of it, either.'

'No, it's not easy. But I don't regret a minute of it. I wouldn't give up Josh for anything on the face of the earth.'

He's a charming child, Jill thought. But does Scott also mean that he's precious because his mother is gone, because he's the only reminder of her? 'You looked at me so strangely a minute ago,' she began hesitantly.

'Did I?' He didn't sound interested. 'I must have been surprised that you had descended to playing with Josh, after everything you've said about kids.'

'That's not fair, Scott. I don't have anything against kids.'

Scott rubbed the back of his neck. 'That's quite a pile of equipment you've got there.' He nodded at the camera and lenses as she set them carefully on the end of the picnic table.

Obviously, Jill thought, we aren't going to talk about his daily life any more, or about my views on children. All right; I can take a hint. 'I think I got some nice pictures of Josh, if it wasn't too dark. Would you like copies, if they turn out?'

He hesitated for such a brief instant that she thought that she might have imagined it. 'I'd like to see them. I thought you spent all your time on the other side of the camera.'

Jill shrugged. 'It's fun to play with images on film, but it's only a hobby.' She pulled the lawn chair around to face him and sat down.

'What do you do with your spare time?'

'There isn't much of it. Modelling isn't exactly easy and glamorous, you know. Besides, I can't eat, drink and be merry very often, because alcohol, rich food and late hours can be poisonous.'

Scott shook his head. 'That doesn't fit with my idea of your life. Dancing and nightclubbing and partying—drawing men like moths to the flame. But you make it sound as if you live in a convent somewhere.'

'Of course I don't. I have my share of admirers.'

'I'll bet you do.' It was dry. 'At least one of them is in the crew you're working with, or I miss my guess.'

'Gareth, you mean? He thinks I'm too old to be interesting any more.' Jill laughed, but it was an effort. 'Not every man finds me attractive, Scott. You've made it quite obvious that you don't.'

'I didn't say that I thought you were unattractive. I would just prefer you with a little more flesh on your bones.'

Like Cassie? she wondered.

'But then I'm only a small-town hick,' he said smoothly. 'Who would expect that I would have any taste?'

This, Jill told herself, is getting us nowhere. Besides, what makes him think my measurements are any of his business? 'Is there somewhere in town I can get my film developed?'

His eyes lit with wry amusement, as if to say that she hadn't fooled him with the change of subject. 'Of course. Give it to me; I'll take it to the store tomorrow.'

'Do you mean your store?'

He nodded. 'Surprised?'

'Is there anything you don't do there, Scott?'

'We don't show movies and we don't cut hair. But just about everything else.'

Jill shook her head in amazement. 'When you said your father ran a hardware store, I certainly didn't picture anything like this.'

There was a long silence. 'Would it have made any difference, Jill?' It was a soft, husky question.

Her heart started to pound erratically, and then she remembered that this was the man who had forgotten her so completely that a year after their break-up he had been married and waiting for the birth of his child.

She got to her feet and picked up the camera so that she didn't have to look at him. 'Scott, don't be silly. Of course it wouldn't have made any difference. We just weren't suited, that's all. I'm glad the store is a success; it obviously is. You're not exactly living in a slum.' She waved a slim hand up at the house.

'It's just the town that's a ghetto, is that what you mean?'

'That's not what I said. Springhill seems to be a perfectly nice little town, for people who like small places. I'd stifle here.'

'A matter of taste,' he said quietly.

'Exactly. I'm glad you understand.'

'Personally, I like being able to park my car on

Main Street with the windows rolled down. I like being able to leave the back door unlocked so that the meter reader can get in without a fuss. Those things are more important to me on a daily basis than theatres and museums.'

'We all have our preferences,' said Jill, with a shrug. She finished winding the film back into its tiny canister and handed it to him.

He dropped it into his shirt pocket and said, 'Would you like another cup of coffee?'

She shook her head.

'Then as soon as Josh finishes his bath I'll take you home.'

It startled her; she looked out across the lawn to the still pink western sky as if to confirm her sense of time. It was early yet; a little voice at the back of her brain said, He's very anxious to get rid of you all of a sudden. Oh, stop it, she ordered herself. She needed an early night, so that she could be on location in the morning. Scott was just being thoughtful. But the suspicion hovered.

She saw that watchful, wary look in his eyes again, and wondered if he had read her mind. 'What did you do with him last night?' she asked. 'When you came back to the motel?'

For a moment, she thought he was going to ask what business it was of hers. 'He was at Cassie's,' he said finally. 'He was asleep when we got home from the party, so I left him overnight.'

'How considerate of him. You needn't trouble yourself tonight, Scott. It's only a little way, and I can walk.'

Scott shook his head. 'A lady alone on the streets after dark—no, I'd feel better if I drove you.'

The hint of gallantry hurt worse than anything else

he had said, mostly, she thought, because he so obviously didn't mean it. 'Do you mean Springhill has a crime rate?' she asked tartly. 'I'd have thought it was perfect, from what you've said.'

He frowned a little. 'Things happen, even in small towns.'

She bent over her camera, fussing with taking a lens off and putting a different one on, mostly to occupy a little time. Hurry, Josh, she thought. Please hurry.

She didn't hear Scott move, didn't know he was behind her until his hand smoothed a lock of her hair back over her shoulder. She jumped a little, startled, and turned her head, and his hands closed on her shoulders to steady her. Then his mouth brushed the velvety triangle just beneath her earlobe, caressing it with gentle fire.

Shake him off, the sane half of her mind ordered. Tell him to stop. Set the camera down and slap him if you have to!

But her traitorous body relaxed against him instead. She heard a tiny, soft animal sigh, and didn't know until his fingers tightened on her shoulders that it was she who had made the sound. He turned her away from the table and into his arms, and his mouth claimed hers, tenderly, but quite as if he had the right to kiss her.

And perhaps he did, she thought muzzily, as her lips softened under his. He had always known precisely how to kiss her so that her brain turned into butter, and he used every ounce of that old knowledge now. There was no element of force about him, and not even a hint of a demand in the pressure of his mouth on hers. But the soft caress of his fingers against the nape of her neck, and the tender tease of his tongue against her lips, and the warm pressure of his body against the length of hers made every cell throb with wanting to please him. It was a sweet agony that soon, very soon, would be eased.

The back door slammed, and by the time Josh was on the patio they were five feet apart. One of Jill's hands clutched the edge of the picnic table; the back of the other one was pressed to her mouth, as if afraid the child might see evidence of that unrestrained kiss.

Scott held out a hand to Josh. 'We're going to take Jill home now,' he said. His voice trembled a little, Jill thought, and he was breathing a little faster than normal. Or was it just her imagination?

Josh's lower lip stuck out, but he didn't protest.

'Thanks,' said Jill. 'But I really can walk.'

Scott didn't look at her. 'I'll take you.'

'I think I'd be safer with the muggers,' she said tartly.

He laughed at that. 'Don't you think Josh will be a good enough chaperone?'

It was just my imagination, she thought. I didn't want to admit that he might be able to kiss me like that and be completely unmoved himself. Well, as he pointed out himself, I'm certainly safe now, with Josh along. I might as well not argue about it.

They went through the house, across the high-ceilinged great room where the remnants of twilight showed the outline of furniture. She had time for only a mere glimpse—not enough to judge the colours or styles—but she couldn't miss the stone fireplace that filled one wall. It was a room to curl up in on a cold night, she thought, when a snowstorm was howling outside, and drink hot chocolate before a snapping fire, and play backgammon or cribbage . . .

At least it could be an inviting room, she thought, if it weren't so confoundedly gloomy. It would be almost impossible to banish the shadows that crept down from the cathedral ceiling. As it was, she thought with a shiver, that room could throw a blight over any kind of entertainment.

She had only a quick glimpse around a corner into the kitchen. At least there was a light there; it reflected off shiny white cabinets and Williamsburg blue tiles. It was a big kitchen, and it looked as if it had at one time been well used. His wife must have liked to cook, she thought. Maddening that she still didn't know the woman's name.

But the kitchen too looked bare. Some copper ornaments here and there, Jill mused, would make all those cold white surfaces sparkle with life, and some old botanical prints on the walls would add interest.

Only then did she realise the direction of her thoughts, and she sternly reminded herself that she was not likely to be asked to act as Scott Richards' interior decorator any time soon.

And I am glad, she told herself.

The house was bigger than she had thought, though—its appearance from the street had been deceptive. Even the view from the patio hadn't prepared her for the expanse of space inside. Far too much house for two people, she thought. But then, when he built it, Scott had probably expected that some day it would be a house full of children.

His car was an almost-new dark blue Cadillac, polished and discreetly luxurious. She sank into the leather upholstery; Josh climbed into the back seat.

Scott tapped a button and the garage door opened with a mechanical groan. He turned round to watch as he backed the car out, and his hand on the upholstery brushed Jill's hair. She stiffened and said suddenly, 'Why did you do that?'

'I always like to see where I'm going.'

'Don't pretend to misunderstand, please. You know I'm talking about the——' She broke off, suddenly aware that Josh had sat up and propped his elbows in the space between the two front seats. He was busily wiggling his loose tooth. 'About what happened on the patio,' Jill said stiffly.

'It was what you expected, wasn't it? You'd have been disappointed if I hadn't done something of the kind.'

It was perfectly calm and logical, and it made her see red. The nerve of the man, to kiss her with the certainty of a lover who was confident that his caress would be welcomed—he would have deserved it if she had slapped him silly!

'Well, did you enjoy it?' she asked tartly.

'Enjoy?' He seemed to turn the question over and think about it. 'Oh, yes, I enjoyed it. Besides, it answered my question, and confirmed what I suspected last night. You may say that you don't have time for much of a social life, Jill—but you certainly haven't forgotten how to kiss.'

She hadn't recovered her voice by the time they reached the motel. He stopped the car under the canopy, and Jill got out without a word. His voice stopped her half-way to the motel door; she turned to see him leaning against the car, his arms folded across his chest. 'Aren't you even going to say thank you?' he asked gently.

'For the dinner? Or am I supposed to be grateful for the kiss?' she asked, without thinking.

Amusement sparkled in his eyes as if candles had been lit behind them. 'If it's the kiss,' he said, 'I could think of a charming way to express your gratitude——'

'Thanks for the steak, Scott,' she said tartly.

He grinned. 'I didn't get a minute of sleep all last night,' he mused, 'because I was regretting that I hadn't taken you up on your invitation.'

'I didn't issue any invitations,' Jill snapped. 'That was a figment of your imagination!'

He didn't seem to hear. 'I was wrong last night, you know,' he said, very softly. 'I do want to make love to you again.'

He was six feet from her, but the warmth of his gaze was so strong that her skin was aching as if he were stroking it.

'That's your misfortune, Scott,' she said shakily. She turned and stumbled into the motel lobby.

But she thought she heard him murmur, as the door closed behind her, 'Is it my misfortune, Jill? Or is it yours?'

She spent half an hour on her make-up and concluded that she had concealed the evidence of a restless night. But Joe Niemann took one glance at her in the soft early light at the edge of the cornfield and said, 'You look like hell, Donovan. Didn't Scott Richards let you get any sleep at all last night?'

'That is a sexist and unnecessary remark,' she snapped back. 'Furthermore, you're not running a Girl Scout camp, and you're not my mother, so you've got no right to enquire what I do with my extra time!'

'When it messes up a shooting session, I do,' he fired back. 'You've always been a good model, Jill, but here you are acting like an amateur. I'm not about to bend the rules for you if it risks the quality of my work!'

He was right about that, and she knew it. 'It's not as if you're shooting close-ups, Joe,' she said, trying

for a conciliatory note. 'And I promise I'll get a good
night's sleep tonight.'

Joe refused to be soothed. 'Just remember this,' he
said. 'There are plenty of other models who'd jump at
this chance. I gave you the job as a personal favour to
Danny, so don't forget it.'

Jill clenched her teeth so hard she wouldn't have
been surprised if they had shattered. A personal
favour, indeed! she raged. Joe made it sound as if he
had had people standing in line wanting this job.

And he probably had, she reminded herself, once
her temper had a chance to cool off. She had worked
with Joe before, but not often; she did owe this job to
Danny, and if she didn't make good, she was risking
his reputation, too. If this campaign was successful, it
could lead to more work for the entire crew. The
company might even contract with the models and use
them in all the advertising to come—including
snowmobiles, she thought with a twinge of distaste,
which they'll probably want to shoot on a glacier in
Alaska in the depth of winter.

Don't worry about it before it happens, she ordered
herself. Just keep your mind on today's shooting.
That alone will give you plenty to think about.

As it happened, however, they didn't even get
started that morning. The cameras were set up, the
field was ready, but as Gareth drove the first all-
terrain vehicle down from the trailer, the ramp gave a
shriek and collasped. The machine, which had been
balanced on the narrow metal track, rolled off the
edge of the ramp and bounced on its side in the dirt.
Gareth managed to jump clear of the vehicle as it slid,
but he landed heavily on a patch of gravel with a
sickening thud. The only thing that moved for an
aeons-long instant was one wheel of the upside-down

all-terrain vehicle, still spinning lazily.

For a moment there was no sound. Then Gareth let out a bellow, and Jill relaxed. It wasn't a scream of pain, but a yell of fury, and she thought that if he could make a noise like that, he couldn't be too badly hurt. Then she reached his side and realised that his leg, under the shreds of his white trousers, was a bloody mess, and his knee was swelling.

'Niemann!' he was screaming. 'You ought to know these damn things are dangerous!'

Joe Niemann was kneeling beside him by then. 'Anybody got any first-aid training?'

Jill shook her head and retreated to the shade beside the van where she was at least out of the way. Her medical expertise extended to calling ambulances and putting cold packs on bruises, and since they had neither a telephone nor a supply of ice, she wasn't going to be much help. She sat down on the ground, her knees up and her arms folded around them. She was trembling a little herself.

Danny came to sit beside her. 'Got the shakes?' he asked comfortably. 'I'm not surprised. But isn't it just like Gareth to scream about safety now that he's turned himself into a pretzel, when yesterday he was razzing you about being chicken, and saying he'd like to drive the thing at top speed?'

Jill shivered. 'He was doing me a favour, Danny. That was my machine he was bringing off the trailer.'

'Well, it's not your fault. And actually it isn't his, either. The ramp failed, that's all. Just bad luck for Gareth that it was him.' He pulled a stalk of grass and chewed on it thoughtfully. 'And bad luck for the rest of us, too. Without a model——' He shook his head.

Without a model, Jill thought, we could be stuck in this town for days on end, unable to work, unable to do anything.

The two technicians came towards the van, supporting Gareth between them. He was hopping on his good leg and swearing in a fluent stream. While the technicians propped him up in the back seat as best they could, Joe Niemann came over to Jill and Danny. 'I hate to leave you two alone out here,' he said, 'but I don't have a choice. Gareth can't wait around while we pack all this stuff up again, and we can't just leave it lying out here.'

'We're ready, Joe,' one of the technicians said.

'We'll be back for you as soon as we can,' said Joe, and climbed into the van without waiting for an answer.

Jill watched until the van's dust died down. 'Why do I get the feeling that we've just been abandoned on a deserted island?'

'Without even a pack of playing cards,' Danny commiserated.

In the next couple of hours Jill would have given a great deal for that pack of cards; she had forgotten that her tote bag with its boredom-fighting supplies was still in the van. She helped Danny pack up the cameras, when it became apparent that the crew wouldn't be back in time to do any shooting, and as they worked she picked his brain on fashion and advertising from the photographer's point of view, more from boredom than any real interest in the subject.

'Are you planning to move to the back of the cameras and try to take over my job?' he asked at last, after he had answered her hundredth question.

'You're the second person in two days who's asked that. Why does everyone seem to think it's time for me to retire?'

'Well——' Danny looked a bit embarrassed, 'I guess just because most girls do when they get close to thirty.'

'This one isn't planning to. Thirty isn't old, Danny, and I haven't lost any of my talent.'

There was a long pause as he cleaned dust off a lens and packed it carefully into its foam-lined case. 'Are you sure it's wise to fight it, Jill? It's tough to compete with the youngsters coming in every day. Most of the girls get tired of it after a while and go on to other things.'

'That's even more reason for a few of us to stay with the job, don't you think?'

Danny didn't answer.

'Here comes the van.' Jill pointed to a cloud of dust a long way down the road. 'That's a relief.'

But it wasn't the van, she saw as it drew closer. It was a dark blue Cadillac, and she had seen it before. If Joe had sent Scott out to get them, she thought with frozen logic, it must be very bad indeed. Gareth must have been hurt worse than any of them had thought.

But as the car drew up beside them, she saw that Joe was in the passenger seat, and she relaxed a little.

'How's Gareth?' she asked as Joe opened the door.

'There's nothing broken, but the doctor sent him back to the motel with pain pills. He'll probably sleep most of the day. If we're lucky, he can work tomorrow; if not——' He shrugged. 'This really tears it, doesn't it? We're already well behind schedule.'

Scott leaned against the front corner of the car. 'Is there anything that would help? Another model, perhaps?'

Joe sighed. 'I'll call the advertising agency. But by the time they could get someone out here, Gareth should be mended. It's not as if he'll be in a cast for weeks or something serious.' He looked around. 'You've got everything packed up? The guys are trying to locate a different trailer, but so far they're having no luck. Thanks for the ride, Scott. Would you take Jill back to town? There's no sense in her sitting here any longer.'

'Of course.' Scott didn't look at her; Jill wondered if he felt the same lack of enthusiasm about giving her a lift as she did about accepting it.

'Better call your agency right away, Jill,' Joe called after her, 'and warn them that we're running behind schedule so they don't book you up.'

She wrinkled her nose. 'It's a little late for that. I'm supposed to do a magazine cover next week.'

'Sorry.' Joe didn't sound it; his voice just seemed tired. He rubbed a hand over his hair and looked at the all-terrain vehicle which still lay upside down in the dirt. 'I was a damn fool to let him drive that machine off the trailer,' he mused.

'It could have happened anywhere,' said Jill. 'Even in the field, if it had hit a rut. Those things are unstable, Joe, and dangerous.'

He grunted assent. 'I know it, but please don't start on me, Jill. Gareth spent the whole trip to town telling me what North Star ought to do with the thing. Don't forget to call your agency—they'll just have to postpone your magazine cover. And take a nap, Donovan.'

'Dammit,' she muttered as she got into the car.

'Didn't you sleep well?' Scott asked solicitously as the Cadillac purred along the gravel road at a sedate speed.

'I slept just fine.' Her tone dared him to argue about it.

'Then what were you swearing about?'

'Because I've got a perfectly good job waiting for me next week and I'll probably lose it because of this fool accident, that's why. Magazines can't wait around to suit a model's convenience, you know—they're on a tight schedule.'

'And you'd rather be doing that than relaxing in Springhill?' he said.

'Has anyone ever told you that you have a wonderful command of irony, Scott? Why did Joe drag you into this, anyway? Doesn't this town have a taxi service?'

'Not this week. The driver's in Dubuque visiting his daughter. Shall I take you to the motel?'

She nodded.

'I don't think Gareth wants to have your cool hand on his fevered brow, you know. He didn't ask for you.'

She glared at him.

'But I'll do my best to make you feel loved,' Scott murmured.

The mere suggestion gave Jill the shivers. He wasn't even looking at her, in fact, and he had made no move to touch her. His hands lay casually across the steering-wheel, long fingers relaxed. She stared at them, remembering.

'You're no gentleman,' she said finally.

'I beg to disagree. I took you back to the motel last night, didn't I?' It was lazy.

She ignored him, but when they reached the outskirts of town, she sat up suddenly. 'I've changed my mind about going to the motel, Scott.'

'You're not going to hold Gareth's hand? Does that mean you're going to take me up on my offer instead?'

'Certainly not. Is there a car rental place?'

'In a manner of speaking. But——'

'I'm tired of being dependent on others for transport all the time.'

'Careful, Jill. You'll hurt my feelings.' But a couple of minutes later Scott parked the Cadillac in front of a car showroom. There was a gleaming new model in the window.

'I said I wanted to rent a car, not buy one,' she reminded.

'With the low opinion you have of Springhill, you surely don't expect me to have a Hertz office in my back pocket. They hire used cars here to people whose own vehicles are in for repair. Sorry, Jill, but what you see on the forecourt is the extent of your choice.'

'Oh. That's fine, then.' She saw him reach for the door-handle, and said hastily, 'You don't have to come in with me. I'm sure you need to get back to the store——'

'I think it would be wise if I came with you. It's more apt to be a fair deal that way.'

'Oh.' Jill was touched, much as she hated to admit it. 'I hadn't thought about needing someone to look out for my interests. That's very thoughtful of you.'

'I didn't mean it would be less expensive for you,' Scott murmured as they crossed the pavement. 'I meant it would only be fair to warn them what they're getting into.'

She would have kicked him in the shin if he hadn't opened the glass door just then and used it for a shield. So she just gave him a cold smile instead.

A salesman came up to them with a gleam in his eyes. 'Ready to trade your Cadillac already, Scott?'

Scott laughed. 'Miss Donovan wants to rent a car for a few days. Something with some weight to it, so it won't slide around on gravel roads.'

The salesman's face fell for a moment. Then he turned to Jill and got his first good look at her as she took her sunglasses off. He cleared his throat and said, unsteadily, 'Yes. Of course. We've got several things we could let you have as a loan—free of charge, of course—since you're just visiting for a few days.'

'See what I mean about fairness?' muttered Scott.

The salesman led the way to the back of the used-car lot and waved a hand at a row of cars. Most of them, Jill decided at first glance, would have fitted right into General Patton's tank corps. 'None of these is exactly what I had in mind,' she said gently. 'I'm quite willing to pay the charges, if I could have something a little more up to date. For instance, that.' She pointed across the lot at a tiny, bright-red MG convertible.

The salesman gulped. 'I'll have to check with the boss——'

'You do that,' Jill suggested sweetly. 'We'll go over and look at it in the meantime.'

The top of the windscreen barely came to Scott's belt buckle when he stood beside the car. He looked it over and then said, with deceptive calmness. 'This thing isn't safe, you know.'

'Do you mean it isn't safe with me, or I'm not safe with it? If you're worried about me damaging the car,' Jill said coolly, 'I have a perfectly valid New York driver's licence.'

'As it happens, I am concerned about you. A few minutes ago you complained to Joe about those dirt-bike things being dangerous, but now you want to drive this——' He shook his head.

'This is a lot safer than the bikes.'

'It's still really just a toy, you know.'

'That's exactly why I want it.'

'But you'll be practically sitting on the road, and it's too small for other drivers to see.'

'I really don't care what you think, Scott. Not everyone wants to drive a cabin cruiser.' She slid behind the wheel. The tiny car was only a two-seater, and he was right about the low-slung seat being less than comfortable for a woman of her height. But it would be great fun to drive it for a few days, anyway, she thought. Having a car in Manhattan would make no sense at all, so she had never owned one. And driving her father's sedate sedan once in a while wasn't much fun, either. The little red convertible would at least put a bit of pep into a week that was otherwise threatening to become the worse nightmare of her life.

The salesman came back, wearing a grin. 'The boss says it's fine,' he announced. 'Since you're a friend of Scott's, that is, and he's vouching for you.'

Jill managed not to laugh at the chagrin on Scott's face; she was very proud of her self-control. He looked, she thought, precisely as if he had just bitten into an apple and found half a worm.

CHAPTER SIX

'DO you mean they actually have telephones out there, Jill? I didn't expect to hear from you at all till you got back to civilisation.' Althea Webb, the head of the modelling agency Jill worked for, had never hesitated to speak her mind.

Jill laughed. 'Someone told one of the technicians yesterday that Springhill is pretty much centrally located in the continental United States, and he said, 'That's right—it's in the middle of nowhere!'

Althea's musical laugh danced across the wires. 'So when is Joe bringing you home?'

'That's why I'm calling.' Jill told her about Gareth's accident. 'So I'm afraid I may not be free to do that magazine cover next week. I suppose they wanted to start shooting on Monday morning?'

There was a brief, barely noticeable silence. 'Don't worry about it, Jill.'

'Do you mean they can actually wait till I get back? That's wonderful!'

'Not exactly.' Something indefinable in Althea's voice sent a frosty pang up Jill's spine. Althea sighed, then said in a rush, 'I suppose there's no easy way to tell you. They've decided against using you at all, Jill. Don't blame the North Star job—even if you were here in New York today, I'm afraid it wouldn't have made any difference.'

Jill tightened her grip on the telephone. 'But why?' she asked blankly. Then she bit her lip; there were any number of reasons, and none of them was a reflection on her abilities. The editor-in-chief might have simply taken a sudden dislike to the idea, that was all; it had happened more than once.

'I'm afraid that they've decided to go for a younger girl, Jill. They think she's more the image that their readers expect.'

'May I ask who they chose?'

Althea's voice was reluctant. 'Kat Hammond.'

'I see. Thanks for telling me, Althea.' Jill swallowed hard and forced herself to say, pleasantly, 'Then I'll tell Joe that it doesn't matter how long the North Star project takes. That will be one worry off his mind, at least.' She put the telephone down carefully and precisely; she would have liked to jerk the cord out of the wall and throw the thing through the window and into the pool, but that would solve nothing.

So Kat Hammond was taking her place on the magazine cover. And not just any magazine, either, but one Jill had longed to occupy, one that had been a dream, a goal, for years. 'Kat Hammond,' she said between clenched teeth. 'It would have hurt less if it had been anyone else.'

For Kat Hammond could have been Jill's younger sister. She had the same oval face, the same strong cheekbones, the same long dark hair. Her eyes were even the same clear green as Jill's. There were differences between them, of course, but in every way that mattered they resembled each other—except, Jill admitted, for one. Kat Hammond had come to the agency just a year ago; she was nineteen years old.

Jill slammed her fist against a pillow. As if that could make me feel better, she thought. I'd like to break the neck of whichever editor suggested me in the first place, and got my hopes up.

Perhaps Danny had been right, she thought.

Younger girls, with fresher faces, were more apt to get the jobs. Was this only the beginning of a long slide in her career, a gradual decline in the number and prominence and importance of her assignments? Would she do better to give up her career gracefully, as he had put it this morning out in that hot cornfield?

'Don't be an idiot,' she told herself. 'It's only one assignment. You've lot a million of them over the years; there were always better ones waiting.'

She gathered up her handbag and wide-brimmed straw hat. Joe's advice to take a nap rang in her mind; fat chance she had of going to sleep, she thought, when she had this on her mind. She'd take the little red convertible out in the country instead, she decided, and drive till she had blown all the cobwebs out of her brain.

She discovered a miniature lake tucked away in the hills twenty miles or so outside Springhill. It lay several miles off the main highway, along a narrow and occasionally twisting gravel road. She almost turned back a couple of times, discouraged about ever reaching her destination, but the signs kept appearing as if by magic whenever she was ready to give up, luring her into going just a little further. Surely, she thought, another mile or so and she would be there. 'I only hope it's worth it,' she muttered. 'Sapphire Lake, how can it possibly live up to that name?'

When the convertible rounded the last curve, though, and she caught her first glimpse of the lake, she felt amply rewarded for the trouble. Crystal-blue water lapped gently at a wide strip of sandy beach and shattered the sunlight into drifting pools of gold and platinum. The lake did indeed look like a flawless sapphire set into a giant's ring and held in place by prongs of towering oaks and pines and maples.

Jill was startled when she saw a couple of good-sized sailing boats on the lake. 'It would take more nerve than I have to manoeuvre a boat trailer down that narrow road,' she muttered.

She could see small houses here and there, nestled into the trees, far enough back for privacy, but each with a view of the water. She had obviously stumbled into a private retreat, she reflected; on a perfect day like this any public beach would be lined with swimmers. But surely, even if she was trespassing on private property, no one would object too much if she just sat quietly for a while and looked at the lake, and thought . . .

At the upper edge of the beach, a tree had fallen, and its trunk lay at an inviting slant. She climbed up on it and sat with her feet drawn up, her arms folded on her knees.

Losing that magazine cover was a blow. Jill's modelling career had always been fairly steady, but it had never hit the highs, the super-star fame and the product-endorsement contracts. It was on that very fact that she was pinning her hopes for continued success; her face was well known, but not so much used that the public or even the advertisers had become tired of it, as sometimes happened to the super-stars.

The magazine cover would have been a tremendous boost to her future work, bringing her to the attention of new advertisers, editors, agencies. It would have helped to prove that Jill Donovan had lost none of her edge, and indeed was getting better with experience. Now, that opportunity was gone. Gone to a woman the very spitting image of herself.

'Don't think about Kat,' Jill ordered. 'It isn't her

fault that they wanted someone younger. She just happened to be there.' And it wasn't the modelling agency's fault either, she told herself. They were in the business of supplying what the customer wanted, not telling them what they should have. And if the customers decided that they no longer wanted Jill Donovan——

'I gave you this job as a personal favour to Danny,' Joe Niemann had flung at her just this morning. It was true, she knew; for this kind of work, which required patience but little skill, there were a hundred models who could fill the position, and Danny had recommended her simply because he liked to work with her.

Or could it be more than that? 'It's tough to compete with the youngsters,' Danny had said. Did he know something that she hadn't seen?

She shivered a little, and realised that clouds were moving in, turning the sapphire lake into a cloudy grey opal. Rain—well, at least it had chosen a day when they couldn't work anyway. It was considerate of Mother Nature to arrange it that way, she thought.

The wind picked up, and waves grew choppy on the western half of the water, leaving the side near her still calm. It was the most intriguing thing she had ever seen. She watched as moment by moment the disturbance crossed the water, till the entire surface of the lake was rolling. She wished she had her camera; it would have been a challenge to capture that moment when the lake had been so neatly split into sunshine and shadow, calm and storm.

She made a mental note to stop somewhere and buy some film, since she had used the last of her supply on Josh last night. I hope the pictures turn out well, she thought. I forgot to ask Scott how long it would take to get them back. Oh, well, it doesn't matter, there's not much doubt that I'll be here, whenever it is.

It had been nice of him to take care of running her errands, though. She would make sure there was a good picture of Josh for him, as a little thank-you, when she left Springhill. A photograph of his son would be something personal and meaningful, not like flowers or a bottle of wine. And it certainly couldn't be misinterpreted, as some gifts could. The last thing she wanted was to let Scott believe that she might have taken him seriously last night, when he had suggested that they should have an affair after all.

The breeze was getting colder, and goose-bumps were rising on her bare arms. She didn't want to leave; it was so peaceful here along the shore. But she could just hear Joe Niemann if she woke up in the morning with a cold, so she reluctantly climbed down from her perch and started back to town.

She didn't particularly want to go to the hardware store for her film, but shopping at another store would be a cheap trick to pull on Scott, after he had taken the trouble to get her last roll developed. She looked warily up and down the aisles when she first went in, but Scott was not in sight, so she sought out the camera department with a lighter heart.

It was more extensive than she had expected, covering everything the well-equipped amateur could desire, and a few more things besides. There was a lens that she had been coveting for months, at a price that was hard to turn down. She had just told the clerk she would take it when a small sticky hand clutched her arm.

'My tooth came out,' Josh announced. 'See?' He dug into the pocket of his shorts and held up a very small, very white, slightly bloody bit of enamel. Then he grinned to show the space where it had been.

Jill admired it dutifully. 'How much did you say that's worth to the tooth fairy?' she asked.

'A quarter, I guess. But I got half a dollar once, for my bottom tooth.' He pointed. 'I was in Arizona when it came out.'

'The cost of living is much higher in the South-West,' Jill said, with a perfectly straight face. 'Even the tooth fairy understands that.'

Josh looked puzzled. The clerk stifled a smile at the exchange and said, 'I'll need your name for the guarantee card, miss.' When Jill gave it to him, he looked thoughtful. 'Donovan—oh, I know why that sounds familiar. You have some pictures ready.' He reached into a drawer and set a large, fat envelope on the counter.

'They can't be,' Jill protested.

'We promise overnight service,' the clerk said proudly. It was indisputably her name on the envelope. But that must mean that Scott had brought her film in last night, after he had dropped her off at the motel.

He probably felt guilty, she told herself tartly.

'Josh! There you are.' There was a note of relief in Cassie's voice as she hurried down the aisle. 'Honestly, child, you can vanish in the space of a blink in this store!'

'I'm sorry,' Josh said politely. 'But I saw Jill, and I wanted to ask if she'd come and play this afternoon.'

'I think Cassie's probably too busy to have me around,' Jill said quickly. She'd just as soon not push Cassie into giving an excuse—or worse, an invitation that she didn't mean.

Cassie shifted the little girl in her arms, and two packages of wildly coloured paper napkins slid out of her grip. Jill caught them. 'Thanks,' Cassie sighed. 'As usual I've left everything till the last minute. Actually, I'd like to have you come over. I don't mean you have to play with Josh, of course, but you can drink coffee and watch while I attempt to ice a birthday cake.'

Jill was startled. There seemed to be nothing but friendliness in Cassie's tone. She would have sworn, after catching the challenging look in the woman's eyes last night, that Cassie would never utter a cordial word to her again, much less renew the invitation to come over for a gossip!

And, if anything, she was even more surprised when she heard herself say, 'I'd like that, Cassie. Thank you.'

A few drops of rain were falling by the time they reached Cassie's house. Josh, securely belted into the passenger seat of the red convertible, looked at the sky with concern. 'Your car is going to get all wet,' he pointed out.

'Then we'll just have to stop and put the top up,' said Jill, with more assurance than she felt. There might be more to driving a convertible than I expected, she thought. If I have my choice, I'd rather not learn how to work the mechanism in the middle of a rainstorm!

But Cassie called to her to put the MG in the garage beside her own car, and Jill heaved a sigh of relief. 'You're a thoughtful girl, Cassie,' she murmured as Josh took her into the kitchen. Cassie had already vanished down the hall to Jamie's bedroom with the sleepy child in her arms.

Rain was pelting against the windows. 'We just made it in time, Josh,' Jill said. 'Look at that!'

Lightning stabbed across the sky and was followed by a particularly deep rumble of thunder. She turned away from the window and realised that his eyes were wide as he watched the sky, and his lower lip was trembling.

Why, he's afraid of the storm, she thought, and he's trying to hide it. Her heart twisted just a little. She wanted to gather him up in her arms and comfort him, but she suspected he wouldn't think that being cuddled was quite the macho thing to do. What was it he had said, about hugs that smothered?

'Would you like to see your pictures?' she asked instead.

'Is that what you've got in your bag?' His eyes lighted.

'It certainly is.' Jill spread the prints out on the kitchen table and held one up to show him. It was the first one she had taken, and at the instant she had snapped the shutter, a couple of the lightning bugs in his jar had been glowing. Unusual, she thought.

Josh looked through the pictures, asked if he could keep one, and went off to play. He seemed to have forgotten the storm, and Jill felt triumphant. She started to sort the photos out so that she could decide which ones to offer Scott.

Cassie had come back in, quietly. 'Did you take that picture, Jill? What a stupid question, of course you must have. It's very good, you know.' She glanced at the array of photographs and picked up one of Josh, stretched on tiptoe, intent on his prey. The lines of his leggy little body were graceful and strong, and the photograph captured the tension of the instant. Cassie stared at it thoughtfully for a long moment, and then looked up at Jill with speculation in her gaze.

'Keep that one if you like,' offered Jill. 'I'm going

to get some extra copies made for Scott too.'

'Thank you.' Cassie put it carefully aside. Then she said, very quietly, 'If you're wise, Jill, you won't let yourself fall in love with him.'

For a moment, Jill wasn't quite sure that she had heard correctly. Finally she said, quite calmly, 'Why, Cassie? Because you want him for yourself?'

Cassie busied herself with the birthday cake, arranging layers on the corner of the table. 'I wouldn't mind, that's sure. He's such an easy child to love,' she murmured. 'But——'

'You're talking about Josh?' Jill's voice cracked in shock.

Cassie looked up in astonishment. 'Who did you think I meant, Scott? For heaven's sake, Jill, I thought you were over Scott years ago—if you ever really loved him at all.'

'I never said I loved him. But tell me what you meant, if you weren't suggesting that you were planning to marry Scott yourself.'

'I just meant that more than one woman over the years has taken a good look at Scott and decided the surest way to his heart was to admire that child, and some of them have been badly burned because of it.'

'Burned—how?' Idly, Jill reached out with a slim finger and mopped frosting from the edge of the cake plate. She sucked it off her finger and looked thoughtfully up at Cassie.

'They didn't realise, until after they'd grown to adore Josh, that Scott doesn't have a heart any more. He buried it with Maria.'

'Maria,' Jill said thoughtfully. Of course, it would be something like that, she reflected. It was a musical name, a beautiful name, a name to whisper into a woman's ear while making love to her.

That's quite enough, she told herself firmly.

Cassie forced pink icing into a plastic bag and began to make rosettes on the edges of the cake. 'There's been an occasional woman, of course,' she said. 'Very discreetly, and usually not around here.'

And he wants me to be the latest in the string, Jill thought. She shrugged. 'I still don't quite see why you're concerned about me, Cassie.'

'Because it would be easy to mistake his intentions. After all, he did propose to you once, didn't he?'

'Yes, but I wasn't planning to hold it over his head,' Jill said drily.

'Good, because he says—and he certainly sounds convincing—that he'll never marry again.' Cassie put the pink icing aside and started to smooth the edges of the cake. 'I think he's just being a hopeless romantic, and it's ridiculous. Scott's a young man, and it's nearly five years since Maria died.'

'She must have been something wonderful,' Jill said slowly, then added thoughtfully, 'or terrible—to make him say that.'

Cassie shook her head definitely. 'Well, she wasn't terrible, that's sure. I didn't know her all that well. They were only building the house when Jim and I moved here, and she died before it was even finished, but she adored Scott, and as for Josh——'

'What happened to her, Cassie?'

'She had been out of town, buying things for the new house, and she drove home in a bad rainstorm. She lost control of the car on the wet road. It was quite a smash.'

'So that's why Josh is afraid of thunder and lightning,' Jill said softly.

Cassie looked at her curiously, then she nodded. 'The odd thing is, I'm almost sure Scott's never told him the details, just that it was a car accident.'

'I wouldn't think you could keep a secret in a town this size. Too many people know what happened.' Jill wiped up another spilled bit of frosting and asked, 'What brought you to Springhill, Cassie?'

'Scott.' Cassie looked up from the icing-tube with which she was writing 'Happy Birthday' on the top of the cake, and laughed at the expression on Jill's face. 'Now you think I've been feeding you a line, don't you? It was indirectly Scott, let's put it that way. Jim's company was looking for a good site for expansion, and Scott was the one who sold them on Springhill. Pure coincidence, really, though I will admit I campaigned to come here too. If I was going to be buried in a small town, I figured it might as well be one where I already knew someone.'

'But now, why do you stay?'

'After Jim left, you mean? Because I like it here,' Cassie said simply. 'Small towns have dreadful reputations for gossip, but they're also the only place on earth where people really do love their neighbours as themselves. When Jamie was sick last winter, a bunch of my friends set up a schedule so there was always someone at the hospital with her, round the clock. Name me a city where that would happen, or where the hospital would let them in.'

'Don't you miss the excitement? The millions of things going on all the time?'

'Not as much as I would have expected. Besides, we have things going on, like birthday parties.' Cassie smiled ruefully. 'I know it doesn't sound like much.'

Jill didn't answer. What could I say, she thought, that wouldn't sound patronising? It sounded deadly dull, but there was no point in saying that!

'There!' said Cassie with relief. She admired the

finished cake and set it carefully aside. 'There's a sort of proverb that I've heard here in Springhill, and nowhere else. People say, "Sweep your own front porch first." Then, if you've any time left over to mind someone else's business, you're more apt to help them than to spread gossip. It's not a bad way to live, Jill.'

Jill shuddered. 'Perhaps. But I couldn't handle it.'

For a moment she thought Cassie looked almost sorry for her. Then she said, 'Would you like to try a new dessert I made? It's called Murder by Chocolate.'

'Sounds too rich for me.'

'Oh, come on. You can certainly stand to risk gaining half a pound. And as for me, I decided a long time ago that I could be thin and irritable all the time, or plump and good-natured. People seem to like me much better this way.'

The time for confidences seemed to be gone, Jill thought. Cassie was chattering cheerfully now, as if she regretted what she had said.

Or, Jill told herself, as if she had accomplished what she had meant to. I wonder, she thought, just what Cassie actually thinks.

When Cassie threw a birthday party, Jill decided some hours later, it was really a party. Jill had assumed that a one-year-old's party would include a handful of toddlers, a few brightly wrapped gifts and some ice-cream to smear over the furniture. Instead, it seemed to her that half the town of Springhill had turned out for the occasion. Most of the people, Jill thought, weren't really there to celebrate Jamie's birthday, but it made a good excuse to get together. She supposed that was what Cassie had meant when she said there was usually something going on in Springhill.

The rain had stopped, but the sky stayed grey and
gloomy and threatening. The heat of the day had
broken, though, and the patio behind Cassie's house was
the most popular gathering-place for the guests. Jill was
sitting there in a comfortable lawn chair after dinner
when Josh came up, breathless and giggling from a game
of tag on the wet lawn, and crept on to her knee.

'Josh, you're all wet,' said Scott, with a frown. 'You'll
get Jill's clothes soaked.'

She scowled at him and drew the child up on her lap.
Why is he upset? she wondered. I haven't done anything
to be concerned about, just offered his son a way to get
warm. 'I've survived being wet before, Scott.' Josh
snuggled against her. His little body felt chilly, and she
put her arms around him to get him warm again.

Scott looked down at her for a long moment, with a
sort of distant look in his eyes, then his expression
warmed. 'Yes,' he agreed, 'I seem to remember.'

Jill swallowed hard and turned her back on him, as
much as she could in the confines of her chair. Scott
laughed and turned to talk to another guest. His hand
rested on the back of her chair; Jill thought it must
appear very casual. But a watcher could not know that
his thumb had crept through the curtain of her hair and
was stroking the nape of her neck.

What am I supposed to do, she thought, jump up and
scream and run away? That would look delightful. The
best thing to do is just sit still. Funny, I never knew
before that the nape of my neck could be so sensitive.

She settled Josh more comfortably against her and put
her cheek down against his sweat-dampened hair,
determined to ignore Scott's antics.

A man carrying a coffee-cup perched on the patio wall
beside her chair. He was in his middle fifites, perhaps,
with short greying hair and a pugnacious chin. 'Miss

Donovan? I'm John Williams, and I own the photo studio here in town. Cassie says you've got some pictures I should see.'

Jill shook her head. There was a humorous twinkle in her eyes. 'Cassie would never dream of asking her lawyer friends to look at her lease over dinner, I'm sure. Why should she inflict my amateur photos on you?'

'Because I saw one on her kitchen counter a minute ago, and I liked it,' he said crisply. 'I wanted to see if you were really good, or if that one was accidental.'

Jill laughed. She liked this man with his blunt style, but that didn't mean she wanted him to pore over her work. 'It was accidental, I'd say. Josh is a natural model. I'd like to see what the cameraman in our crew could do with him. He used to do quite a bit of work with child models.'

Scott's thumb stopped making its slow, erotic circles on the nape of her neck. 'Don't plan on turning my kid into some sort of plastic doll just because you think that's a normal way of life,' he said. His voice was low and absolutely level.

Jill's eyes were wide with shock as she looked up at him. His jaw was tense, and she had never heard him speak in that tone before.

'It's not as if I'm trying to sign him to a contract, Scott,' she protested. 'I just said I thought Danny could get some wonderful pictures.'

'I absolutely refuse to permit it. Is that plain and simple enough for you?'

'What's eating you all of a sudden? It was only idle conversation, Scott. Danny's far too busy with his job to play around, anyway.'

'Good.' It was uncompromising.

It made her even more furious. 'If you don't want pictures taken of Josh, I'm surprised that you didn't

confiscate my film last night and tell me it had got lost in
the lab!'

'That was a little different,' said Scott. 'You're not a
professional.' He turned on his heel and went into the
house.

John Williams' eyebrows had risen during the
exchange.

'See?' said Jill, trying to pass it off as a joke. 'You've
now got a first-hand opinion that I'm not very good.'

Josh was wriggling about on her lap. 'What's the
matter with you?' Jill asked with a trace of exasperation.

He turned big brown eyes, full of horror, upon her. 'I
can't find my tooth!' He had pulled his pocket inside
out, and sure enough the tiny bit of enamel was gone.
He started to sob.

Jill looked around in desperation. Wasn't that just like
Scott, she thought, to have nagged at her about nothing
and then vanished just at the moment she needed him?
He could put a stop to the tears and soothe Josh's
heartbreak, that was for sure.

And so can you, she thought, if you've just got enough
sense to think about it calmly. There was no chance of
finding the tooth; Josh might have dropped it anywhere.

She pulled the child closer. 'Well then,' she said
comfortably, 'we'll just have to write the tooth fairy a
note, and tell her what happened.'

There was a sob, and a sort of hiccup, and then
silence. 'Will she believe me?' Josh asked pathetically.

'Of course she will. There's a great big gap in your
mouth, isn't there? We'll tell her we think it's lost in
Cassie's back yard, and with her magical powers, I'll bet
she can find it with no trouble at all.'

Josh sat up suddenly and slid off her lap. 'Let's do it
right now,' he urged.

Jill rose. 'Sorry, Mr Williams,' she said, 'but I think

my pictures will have to give way to more urgent matters.'

He laughed. 'Besides,' he said, 'you didn't want to show me, anyway.'

'There's paper in the playroom,' Josh announced. 'You can write the letter, and I'll draw a picture of my tooth so that she knows what it looks like.'

The playroom was at the far end of Cassie's house. Josh dragged her down the hallway, past Jamie's room and a cosy little den. The door of Cassie's bedroom was half closed; as Josh tugged her past it, Jill heard voices from inside.

'Ridiculous, isn't it?' a woman said shrilly. 'The way she's making up to that child. And poor Josh doesn't even know he's being used.'

'Well, she'll be disappointed,' a different voice, lower, more cultured, replied. 'Better women than she is have tried that trick, with no success. It's sweet, I think, how he's still so devoted to Maria, after all these years. He loved her so very much, you know.'

It was a ghastly echo of what Cassie had said that afternoon. The blood drained from Jill's face, and she stood frozen in the hallway for a long moment, heedless of Josh's impatient tugs at her hand.

It's not true, she wanted to scream. I'm not using Josh. I'm not playing games with him, or using him to get close to Scott! There's nothing I want less than to be involved with Scott again.

I want to make love to you again, he had said.

And what about me? she thought. Is that what I want too? Is that why I get the shivers whenever I'm close to him? Am I just one of those foolish women Cassie told me about, after all?

CHAPTER SEVEN

JILL helped Josh write his note and watched as he crayoned a colourful border around the edges of the paper, listening with only half an ear to his chatter about what he would do with the twenty-five cents he was almost certain to find under his pillow tomorrow morning.

Josh was a delightful child, Jill thought; Cassie was right about that. But it was one thing to allow a six-year-old's company to beguile the boredom of a day of enforced leisure, and it was something else to want anything more than that. I must have gone a bit berserk when I heard those women talking, she thought. I have no hidden motives, and to let their accusations make me wonder for even an instant is insane.

Of course, she understood why they had suspected something of the sort. Any unmarried woman in Springhill would certainly be tempted by the combination of Scott and Josh Richards. There weren't many unattached men in a community this size, and when you added the advantages presented by Scott's business, to say nothing of his sheer dark attractiveness, just the memory of his bronzed and dripping body could curl a woman's toes, she thought, remembering how he had looked last night when he had pulled himself out of the pool. It was no wonder that he had been pursued.

Of course those women had assumed that Jill must be trying to snare him. Foolish as it was, she thought, those women were incapable of understanding that to a woman like Jill Donovan, not even Scott could be worth the loss of a career, of the city life she loved, of the world outside this tiny little town.

Not even Scott, she repeated to herself. Now just what had made her say it that way?

Josh folded the finished note into a tiny wad and thrust it at her. 'Keep this for me,' he said. 'So I don't lose it.'

She tucked the note into the pocket of her jeans as they walked down the hallway, back to the party. 'I hope I don't forget about it when you're ready to go home,' she warned him. 'It would be pretty silly if the tooth fairy left a quarter under *my* pillow tonight!'

Josh giggled and tugged at her hand till she bent down beside him. Then he flung both arms around her neck and put a wet kiss on her cheek. 'You're awfully nice,' he said.

It was quite the best compliment Jill had ever received, and it made her feel just a little wobbly inside. She ruffled his hair and sent him off to eat his cake and ice-cream, and she stood by the kitchen door for a long moment watching him, with a tender little smile.

When she looked up, it was to find Scott's gaze focused on her, from across the room. There was a sort of cautious wariness in his eyes.

As if he's afraid that he's being hunted, she thought irritably. Did Scott, too, believe that she was pursuing him? The very idea that he might be thinking something of the sort made her angry, because it was so far from the truth. He was the one who had suggested that they have an affair, for heaven's sake! As though she would seriously consider such a thing.

Of course being around him was enough to tease old

memories back into uncomfortable life; there was no escaping that. He had been an incredible, a wonderful lover, teasing and tender by turns, able to mould her moods, to shatter her with the ecstasy of his lovemaking. Those things were not easily ignored.

But that didn't mean she wanted to repeat the experience. It would be sheer foolishness to get involved with him again. She had a job to do, and memories couldn't be allowed to interfere with that. Besides, in another few days, when Gareth was well and the photographs were taken, they would pack up and go back to the city, and she would never see Springhill, Iowa, or Scott Richards again.

And it can't come a minute too soon for me, she thought, then sighed, and went back out on the patio to sit by herself.

The setting sun fought its way between the storm clouds that still hovered over the town, and its light turned them to angry pink, and then to champagne, and then to gold. Jill sat and watched the shifting silhouettes of the huge old trees against the clouds, without giving a thought to the passing of time or the chilling of the air, until the sun's brilliant palette was gone and only sullen grey remained.

That beauty, at least, was something positive to take home from this trip, she thought. It wasn't often that she got the chance to see a magnificent sunset in New York; there were too many buildings in the way, and too many days when her work schedule didn't allow time to simply sit and watch.

By the time she finally stirred, it was nearly dark, and her muscles had tightened from the long minutes of sitting absolutely still. When she came back into the house, the last of the guests were saying goodbye. Jill looked at her wristwatch in surprise—no, it wasn't terribly late, she reassured herself. She reached into her pocket for her car keys and came up with a folded bit of paper instead. It was Josh's note to the tooth fairy.

But Josh and Scott were nowhere to be seen.

It was almost a blow that neither of them had sought her out to say goodnight. She knew Scott had been upset when he said that he would not allow Danny to take pictures of Josh, but she had had no idea that he was so angry that he would leave without even speaking to her.

You should be glad, she thought. At least he won't be renewing his invitation to go to bed with him.

But that left her with a problem; she did have a piece of Josh's property, and she suspected he might be unhappy about forgetting it. There was really only one thing to be done, Jill told herself with a shrug. And if the last of the departing guests saw her knocking on Scott's front door, and assumed that she was still chasing him—well, that was their problem. Everybody who mattered knew it wasn't true.

She had rung the bell twice before Scott answered the door. 'I'm trying to deal with a bath and a tantrum all at once,' he said, with a harried note in his voice, 'so if you don't mind waiting——' A peal of sobs resounded from the top of the stairs.

Jill held out the bit of paper. 'I think this might take care of the tantrum.'

He took it cautiously. 'It may, at that. He's been telling me that a substitute just wouldn't do.'

'I forgot I had it,' she said, a little awkwardly, but feeling that some sort of explanation was necessary. It wasn't as if she wanted to be there, after all, and she was darned if she wanted him to think she had planned this.

'Josh forgot it too, till he was brushing his teeth. Then the world came to an end, as far as he was concerned. Pour yourself a glass of wine.' Scott pointed towards the kitchen, then vanished up the stairs, and a moment later the sobs died.

Jill stood in the front hall, shifting uneasily from one foot to the other, uncertain of what she wanted to do. Despite the invitation, she didn't feel entirely welcome. Actually, she thought, he had sounded more as if he was issuing an order.

Her errand was done; she might as well go. But wouldn't it be awfully rude just to walk out? And if he was truly angry about the modelling business, perhaps she should try to explain.

She was still standing there when Scott came back. 'Sorry,' he said. 'I should have told you where to find everything.'

She followed him into the kitchen. 'I didn't expect to stay, you know.'

The cork slid out of the bottle with a refined little pop, and he filled a pair of long-stemmed glasses and handed her one.

'I make it a rule not to drink alone,' he said. 'And after a tucking-in like tonight, believe me, Jill, you're performing an important public service to have a glass of wine with me.'

She laughed, suddenly reassured. Whatever had been bothering him, he had apparently put it behind him. And she didn't really want to go back to that dull motel room. It was early yet. 'One glass,' she agreed.

He led the way into the great room and snapped on a couple of lamps before dropping on to the couch and stretching out his feet.

Jill curled up on the other end, where she could see him. He looked exhausted, every muscle in his body lax, his eyes closed, the glass held loosely between two fingers. She half expected him to drop it at any minute.

She took advantage of the opportunity to study the room. It looked a little different tonight, with the lamps casting their pools of golden light. There were still plenty of shadows in the upper reaches of the cathedral ceiling, but it was an intimate sort of dimness tonight, not a frightening one. The expanse of golden oak floor gleamed, interrupted only by the scattered area of rugs that divided the huge room into comfortable spaces.

It was obviously a room that was lived in—no company-only parlour, this. On the stone hearth a set of intricate building-blocks had been half assembled into something that looked like a construction crane. On the coffee-table, on top of a brown paper bag with *Springhill Hardware* lettered on the side, lay an assortment of tools and an electrical switch still in the plastic package. On each side of the fireplace, bookshelves were stuffed to bursting, and here and there the light caught against a tooled leather binding, pushed in beside a gaudily jacketed best-seller. The room was obviously clean, but Jill's fingers itched to bring a little order to the mess.

'My cleaning lady comes tomorrow,' Scott said lazily.

She jumped and turned to stare at him. To all appearances, he hadn't moved or even opened his eyes at all.

'I didn't mean to imply——' she began stiffly. Then she caught herself when she saw the smile tugging at the corners of his mouth. 'You're very lucky to have a cleaning lady who's an electrician on the side,' she said coolly. 'I suppose she actually washes windows too.'

He grinned. 'If I leave the switch there, I'll remember to put it in tomorrow before I go to work.'

'Quite a system.'

'It works. Of course, it drives the female mind to madness.'

'Is that why you asked me in? To show me how impossible it would be to change your ways?'

'Were you thinking of trying to do it?' he countered lazily.

Jill could have cheerfully bitten off her tongue, knowing that she had given him the reaction he had hoped for. 'Of course not. I haven't any desire to change you.'

'I've always known you were a rare woman, Jill.'

She took a deep breath and went on as if he hadn't interrupted. 'Because I wouldn't want you, no matter what.'

'Refreshing,' he murmured.

Curiosity made her say, 'Doesn't it bother you that half the people who were at the party tonight think that I'm laying a trap for you?'

He shrugged. 'I learned a long time ago that it doesn't much matter what a single man does in a small town. Especially a man whose wife died. He will be talked about.'

Jill shivered delicately. 'That's a bit morbid.' She sipped her wine. 'All the old ladies will be greatly relieved to see me driven away in disgrace.'

Scott smiled, without looking at her. 'They'll probably think I was very smart not to let you catch me,' he said agreeably.

'And they'll never know that the truth was exactly the opposite,' she said lightly.

He turned and propped his elbow on the back of the couch, and studied her, his gaze lingering on the rapid rise and fall of her breasts under the thin shirt. 'Is it?' he asked.

'You can't think I'm on the prowl, Scott. If I were, I'd have jumped at your offer of an affair.'

'There are more effective ways, sometimes.'

It brought back the memory of the two voices in Cassie's bedroom. Jill drank half her wine and said, flatly, 'But you must know that I would never do anything to injure Josh, don't you, Scott?'

'I'm sorry I snapped at you,' he said. 'It just hit me wrong.'

'He's a darling child, and I wouldn't dream of hurting him. I simply wasn't thinking when I said that Danny should photograph him—I certainly didn't mean to make him a model. Heaven knows I've seen what happens when children are pushed like that.'

He looked at her enquiringly.

'Too many times the parents are interested in the glory and money for themselves, not in what happens to the child,' she said. 'The competition is terribly harsh, and it can be devastating when a job falls through.' She finished the last swallow of her wine and shook her head when Scott looked questioningly at the empty glass.

Why am I telling him all this? she asked herself. Scott certainly doesn't care! But she couldn't seem to stop herself. 'It's especially hard for a child who isn't old enough to make his own decisions.'

'You're not just talking about children, though, are you?' It was very gentle.

His voice, she thought. I could drown myself in his voice, when he's being kind. Her eyes grew a bit moist. 'No.' Her voice trembled a little.

Scott sat up straight and turned to study her. 'Something's happened, hasn't it? It's more than the accident today. That upset you, but not like this.' There was a direct, compelling look in his brown eyes that demanded an answer.

She tried to laugh it off. 'Oh, just the normal foul-ups,' she said. 'It's nothing major, really. They hired someone else to do the magazine cover I was supposed to pose for, that's all.'

'Because you won't be back in time?'

Jill paused. 'No,' she whispered finally. 'It wasn't that at all.' She braced for the next question, and cursed herself for being a fool. Why didn't you just nod? she asked herself. You don't owe Scott any explanations. It wouldn't really have been a lie.

'Why is it so important?' he asked. 'You've been on other covers.'

She dashed tears away with an unsteady hand and said, 'That's different, you know. Not at all like this one. The one that's on the stands this month is only a small magazine, with regional circulation. The one I was supposed to have is read all over the world. It could have meant jobs in Europe——'

'Is that what you want, Jill?'

'Of course it's what I want! You don't think I like the kind of thing I'm doing at the moment, do you? This is just something to do to pay the rent while I wait for the really important things.'

He didn't say anything at all for a long moment, and when he did, she was astounded to find not the slightest hint of sarcasm in his words. 'It's a tough life, isn't it, Jill?'

She nodded. 'Most people don't understand that, you know, they think it's all very glamorous. The travel, the wonderful clothes—they don't understand that we don't own the clothes, and that we can't borrow them as we please, either. And as for travel——'

'Instead of romantic Maui, you sometimes get Springhill, Iowa,' he said.

'More often than not, lately,' she admitted, then forced herself to laugh. 'It's all part of the job.' For a moment she was quite sure that she had convinced him, until she looked straight at him and saw the compassion in his eyes.

Her first reaction was anger that he dared to feel sorry for her, and then the pain that she had been trying so hard to bury since she had talked to Althea that afternoon welled up inside her till there was no forcing it back into the hidden spaces. She gritted her teeth in a vain attempt to keep her lips from trembling. 'I wanted that cover so very much, Scott.'

He reached a long arm out for her, and settled her head comfortably against his chest. 'Come on and cry it out,' he said. 'You'll feel better.'

As if I were no older than Josh, Jill thought resentfully. As if my troubles were no more important than a child's.

But there was something about the strength of that arm, and the steady thumping of his heart under her ear, and the spicy sharpness of his aftershave lotion, that seemed to paralyse her and make it impossible to pull away. One tear sqeezed painfully past her tightly closed eyelids and soaked into his thin shirt, and then another, and then the flood began.

He didn't say anything, just held her warmly and strongly, and stroked her temple with his fingertip. Finally that small hypnotic movement reached her and soothed her, and when he finally moved and shifted her slightly away from him, she almost protested. She let her head fall back against his shoulder and looked up at him through half closed eyes.

He's going to kiss me, she thought, as if I were a child to be comforted and then distracted from my troubles.

But she didn't have enough energy to worry about it, so she let her eyes drift shut again and waited.

There was a sudden thump from upstairs, as if a small boy's feet had hit the floor, and every muscle in Scott's body seemed to tense for an instant. But only silence followed.

Jill drew a little away from him. 'That's the story of our lives, isn't it?' she said, with an effort to be cheerful. 'Listening for small noises. Remember the night you sneaked me up the fire escape and into your room at the fraternity house, and we were both terrified we'd be caught?'

For a long moment, she thought he hadn't even heard. Then he sighed. 'Of course I remember,' he said slowly. 'That was the first time we ever made love.'

She stared up at him with dilated eyes. It felt as if a giant hand had clenched around her chest and was crushing her slowly into oblivion.

With one quick jerk, Scott dragged her across his lap till she lay cradled in the curve of his arm, off balance and unable to support herself. A hasty hand pushed the black stream of hair back from her face, and he bent his head to take her mouth in a harshly demanding kiss.

She sagged against him. The instinctive urge to fight him was smothered like a snuffed candle flame by the fierce dominance of that kiss. Deep inside her a primitive blend of aching and exaltation, a feeling that for so long had been only embers, flared to life. She had banked that blaze long ago, and told herself that it was dead. But she had lied, and now she knew that only he could soothe this horrible ache. For a little while, at least, he could ease the pain and give her peace, until she started wanting him once more.

For a long moment she gave herself up to the sheer joy of tasting him, of touching him.

'It's only a few days, Jill,' he said thickly. 'That's all we have. Please, let's make the most of it.' And he kissed her again, as if he knew that mere words could not possibly hold the persuasive impact that his kisses did.

My God, she thought. It's never gone away, and it never will. This longing for him, this hunger only gets stronger with time.

And what happens to me a few days from now, she thought, when my work is done, and I go? A few days, he said. That's all we can have, and that's all he wants. But what about me?

I want him, she thought. I want him so badly—but not just for a few days. That would destroy me, and yet I can't have anything more than that. So it would be better to stop now, no matter how great the frustration and the pain, rather than to face an even worse pain later.

With a wrench that threatened to rip her heart in half, she moaned, 'Scott, no. This isn't right.'

She hardly recognised his voice, harsh with passion, as he said against her lips, 'But how can anything that feels so wonderful be wrong?' His hand tugged her thin shirt free from the waistband of her jeans and slid beneath it to press urgently against her breast.

Against her will, she cried out with the pleasure that the warmth of his palm brought to the sensitive skin. His eyes flared with a sort of triumph, and it took the last of her willpower to whisper, 'Please, Scott, no.' Her voice cracked, and she closed her eyes tight, unwilling to see what might lie in the depths of his.

Very slowly, his hold on her relaxed, and she collapsed, still half lying across his lap, unable to get a grip on anything that might allow her to shift herself out of this humiliating, helpless position. She turned her face into a cushion so that she didn't have to look at him. She could hear something that sounded almost like a rasping sob. Why didn't Scott make it stop? she wondered, and it took a long moment to realise that it was only her own panting breath that she was hearing.

'Why?' he asked harshly. 'Why?'

'Because we've made that mistake once before,' she whispered. 'We were foolish enough once to think that our hunger for each other was love.'

He removed her from his lap with a single movement that was almost a push, and strode across the room to stare out at the wind-tossed trees. He was struggling for breath too, and she thought she had never seen any man so furious in her life. She watched him for a long moment, half afraid of him, and when he turned towards her with the anger gone from his eyes, she released a breath she didn't even know she had been holding.

'Fortunately for us,' he said heavily, 'we're not foolish enough to believe in love any more.'

It staggered her for a moment. Then she nodded. 'That's right.'

Scott came across the room to her. 'Then stay with me tonight,' he said. 'You're right about the hunger, you know. You can't hide from that, Jill. You want me and I want you, and since there's no question any longer of either of us mistaking it for love, why shouldn't we be honest about what we feel and go to bed together?'

'I'd better leave,' she said uncertainly.

'Don't.' It was harsh. 'Please don't.' He didn't move to touch her, but his voice was like a steel web that had reached out to hold her fast.

Her hands clenched till her fingernails cut ridges in her palms, as she fought the magnetic attraction, the memories of his lovemaking. She could escape her questions and her fears in his bed tonight, she knew. How horribly easy it would be to give in! But when tomorrow came——

'I have to go,' she said, and her voice quavered.

He looked at her for a long moment and then turned back to the window, staring out into the darkness.

Jill picked up her handbag and her straw hat. I can't just walk out without another word, she thought. Not with this chasm lying between us. 'Don't—don't forget about the tooth fairy,' she said at last.

His voice was deadly cold. 'I wasn't planning to.' He didn't turn around.

'Goodnight, Scott.' And that, she told herself, was just about the most stupid and inane remark she could have come up with to end an evening like this! The only thing worse would be to wish him pleasant dreams.

'It's raining again,' he said dully. 'You'd be soaked in seconds if you went out in this. I suppose you left the top down on the convertible.'

'Yes, but it's still in Cassie's garage.' That was plenty stupid, she told herself. Cassie ought to get a real kick out of Jill barging in at just past midnight to get her car! She looked out at the storm; the rain was blowing almost sideways, and it rattled as it struck the big windows in sheets.

'It's foolish to drive in this,' said Scott. 'You can't

see fifty feet. Anything might happen.'

She was stunned by the haunted expression in his eyes. It must have been a night like this one when Maria died, she realised.

'Wait till it calms down, Jill, and I'll go over with you and put the top up.' He turned from the window and said heavily, 'Don't worry, I'll behave myself in the meantime. You've made yourself plenty clear, and rape was never my idea of a good time.'

He doesn't want me here, she thought, but he can't bear to send anyone out in this kind of weather. I'm not anxious to go out in it, either. Surely in a few minutes it will ease and I can get away.

She nodded slowly, and groped for something to break the silence with. 'I've got those pictures of Josh,' she offered tentatively. 'You said you'd like to see them.' She dug the envelope out of her handbag with trembling hands and pushed magazines off the coffee-table so that there was space to spread them out.

Scott pulled a chair around and sat down. He gave the photographs a long and searching look, then shook his head. 'No, thanks.'

It cut Jill to the quick. Was there nothing there that appealed to him? I know I'm only an amateur, she thought, but I believed I was a little better than that. At least I didn't embarrass myself tonight by showing them to the guy who owns the studio. He'd have been hard pressed not to laugh.

The telephone shrilled, and Scott leaped for it, as if, she thought, he was eager to seize any opportunity not to have to look at her. 'The alarm's been tripped at the store,' he said when he put it down.

'A burglar alarm, you mean? Who would be out committing crimes on a night like this?'

'Probably no one, it's no doubt a malfunction because of the storm, but I'll have to go and check on it. Sorry I can't help with the car.'

'What do you do with Josh when something like this happens?'

'Bundle him up and drop him off at Cassie's.'

'And then pick him up again in half an hour? That's ridiculous, Scott.'

'So what else do you suggest I do? Leave him alone?'

'Of course not. But there's no point in waking everyone up tonight, when I'm already here.'

He frowned. 'You mean you'd watch him?'

'Don't get any ideas, Scott,' warned Jill. 'It's not that I'm desperate for an excuse to stay. I just think that any child who can sleep through this storm deserves to be left in peace in his own bed.'

'I can't argue with that. I'll be back in a few minutes, anyway.'

She stood in the darkened front hallway and watched the Cadillac's wheels spin the kerb-deep water into high arcs, all the way down Clearview Court. He had been right about visibility, she thought, and was glad that she hadn't taken the tiny MG out in this.

What a night! she thought. Between the thunderstorm outside and the purely human one that had raged within this room, it had been an exhausting evening. My God, she thought, whatever made me come into this house? Why didn't I just hand him Josh's note and get out? Am I some sort of suicidal personality, that I put myself into this position?

At least, she reminded herself, I had sense enough not to make love with him. That would have been the final straw——

Or could he actually be right in saying that, since

love had no place in this unexpected intersection of their lives, there was nothing wrong with indulging their desire? She had forgotten that it was possible to want him so much, so desperately that nothing else seemed to matter.

She thought for a moment that the storm was easing a little, but when she walked over to the windows again she realised that the wind had merely shifted so that the rain wasn't striking full against the glass. She stood there for a long time, remembering what it had been like in those long-ago days when they had played at loving. Could it be that way again, for just a little while?

When the telephone rang again she nearly screamed at the unexpectedness of it. She looked at it for a long moment, wondering who could be calling at this hour. It was certainly someone who would be shocked if she answered. And yet she couldn't just let it ring.

To her relief, it was Scott. 'It's a lot worse than I thought,' he told her. 'The roof is leaking, and I've got water going everywhere. I think you'd better call Cassie, and then just bundle Josh up.'

'Don't be silly,' she interrupted.

'It may take most of the night,' he warned.

'That's all right. I'll nap on the couch.'

There was a momentary silence. 'Jill—thank you.' It was a husky, tender whisper, and it sent shivers of painful pleasure shooting through her veins.

'Don't mention it,' she said, with deliberate coolness. 'I'm not doing anything especially brave, you know. I feel quite safe here as long as you're gone.'

Was that a rueful laugh? she wondered, but the sound was gone before she could quite identify it.

'Jill,' he said, a little sheepishly. 'One more thing. Will you stand in for the tooth fairy? There's some change on the top of my dressing-table in the back bedroom.'

She found his bedroom without any trouble, but she stood outside the door for a long moment before she gathered the nerve to go in. Would he have brought her here, she wondered, and made love to her, if she hadn't regained her senses? Would he have had the gall to bring her to the room he had shared with Maria?

But hadn't Cassie told her that Maria had never lived here, that the house hadn't been finished when she died? Oh, what difference does it make? Jill asked herself, and pushed open the door.

It was a big room, opening on to a balcony that overlooked the pool. The furniture was sparse—a chair, the dressing-table, a king-sized bed. Either Scott liked to sprawl, she thought with a rigid attempt at humour, or Cassie was right and he occasionally sneaked a lady past Springhill's gossips, after all.

Get the quarter for Josh and get out, Donovan, she ordered herself. She found the pile of coins and in an elfin humour picked up a Susan B. Anthony dollar instead. It was just the size of a quarter, after all, and Scott hadn't told her how much money to put under Josh's pillow. If Jill Donovan was going to play tooth fairy, she was going to do it right!

She peeped into Josh's room. It was thoughtful of Scott to leave a nightlight burning, she decided, and tiptoed in. It was harder than she had imagined possible to find a folded bit of paper under a sleeping six-year-old's pillow and substitute a coin, but finally it was safely done and she was back downstairs, feeling just as proud of her daring as if she had successfully broken into Fort Knox.

Too bad, she thought, that she wouldn't be around in the morning to see Josh's face when he discovered his treasure. Or his father's . . . She started to laugh, then found herself yawning in the middle of the giggles. It was past midnight, she realised, and she hadn't slept well for a couple of nights. She looked doubtfully at the long couch.

It wasn't uncomfortable, exactly, she concluded a few minutes later as she turned over and punched a sofa cushion into a shape it had never been intended to take. At least it was long enough for her to stretch out on, and the rain formed a kind of hypnotic pattern that lulled her. But the evening had turned chilly, as if fall was already in the air, and a light blanket would certainly help. She sat up and looked around for something to keep her warm.

A sudden crack of thunder that sounded as if it came from directly above the house jolted her to her feet, and an instant later she heard a frightened cry from upstairs. It was no wonder that crash had wakened Josh, she thought.

An instant later the power went off. A flash of lightning guided her up the stairs and to Josh's door. He was sitting in bed, huddled under a blanket.

'Daddy?' he called. His voice was slow and slurred, as if he had been jolted out of a deep sleep, but wasn't really awake yet.

'I'm here, Josh.' Jill groped her way to his bed in the darkness and sat down on the edge of it. Her fingers found his softly tousled hair and began to stroke it comfortingly. 'It'll be all right.'

'Mommy,' he murmured, and leaned against her with a sigh.

CHAPTER EIGHT

FOR one harsh, shattering moment, Jill found herself wishing that it had been true. The soft hair under her fingertips, the trusting little head pressed against her breast, as if Josh was confident that she could keep away the demons of thunder that had frightened him so—— She wanted to sit there beside him forever and comfort him.

I should have been your mother, Josh, she wanted to say.

Then the longing deep in her soul changed, in the space of a single heartbeat, into self-loathing. She had been so proud of herself tonight, of her clean motives, of her honesty. She would never dream of using Josh, she had told herself. She had even boasted to Scott that she had only Josh's best interests at heart, that of course she would never hurt a child.

And all the time, she had been lying to herself. For what was this, if it wasn't hurting him? Perhaps she hadn't done it on purpose, but her actions had certainly enouraged him to become attached to her. What would happen to Josh when she left Springhill?

She dragged herself back to reality with an effort. You're not so powerful that you could ruin a little boy's life in the space of a few days, Jill, she told herself. Especially not a little boy who has such a close relationship with his father. In a few weeks, he won't even think about you. In a year, when someone says your name, he'll wrinkle his nose and say, 'Was that the lady who wrote to the tooth fairy for me?'

And the truth is, she added brutally, he's not even completely awake right now. He's only half aware that it was the storm that woke him; he might even have been dreaming of his mother, and so when a woman came into his room, of course he called her 'Mommy.' He would have said the same thing to any woman who happened to be here tonight. You're nothing special, Jill Donovan. You're only an incident in his life—and in his father's too, and you would be very wise to remember that.

The lights came back on. After the impenetrable blackness, the sudden glow of the night light on Josh's bedside table seemed to Jill like a searchlight glaring straight into her eyes, stripping bare every secret of her heart.

The child rubbed his eyes and sat up straight. 'Hi, Jill.' He yawned. 'Where's Daddy?'

He doesn't even remember what he said, she thought, with a sudden flood of relief. He doesn't even realise what he called me. It will be all right.

'Your daddy had some trouble at the store,' she said softly. 'I told him I'd stay with you till he got home.'

Josh lay back on his pillows. 'It's an awf'ly loud storm,' he observed.

Lightning was flickering through the curtains with eerie regularity, Jill saw. 'It has no consideration for people who are trying to sleep, does it? I'm sort of glad you woke up to keep me company.'

He looked up at her unbelievingly. 'You were scared?'

'Not scared, exactly. But it's easier to forget about the storm when there's something else to do, and I was getting sort of bored downstairs. It would be very thoughtful of you to let me read you a story before you go back to sleep.'

He grinned. 'All right! Over there.' He sat up again
and pointed to the bookcase built into the corner of
his room. 'I've never had a story in the middle of the
night before.'

'It's the very middle, too. Just past two o'clock.' Jill
hadn't realised until she looked at her wristwatch that
it was so late. She wondered how Scott was doing with
the roof leak down at the hardware store, and how
long it would be before he returned. 'Any special
story?'

'You choose,' Josh offered generously.

The bookcase was like the one downstairs—stuffed
nearly to bursting. She didn't realise until she was
standing next to it, though, that there was one place,
in the very middle of the top shelf, that wasn't
crammed with volumes. It held a silver frame, and
smiling out from it was a fair-haired young woman
with a narrow triangle of a face, and a tiny blanket-
wrapped bundle in her arms.

Jill's fingers squeezed the cover of a picture book
until her knuckles turned white. So this was Maria!

Her first thought was, Josh looks incredibly like
her. Scott must see the resemblance every day, every
time he looks at his son. I wonder if he searches out
the similarities, and treasures them.

None of your business, she reminded herself. What
Scott thinks about it is certainly not your concern.

She looked curiously at the photograph. Maria's
looks had not been outstanding, she thought, or at
least this picture hadn't captured any particular
beauty. But there was a sort of glow about her as she
held her tiny son that made her more attractive than
the most perfect facial structure could have done.

Is there a magic about motherhood? Jill wondered.
They say every bride is beautiful on her wedding day;

does every mother wear that exquisite glow the first time she holds her child in her arms? And did that explain why Scott had said he would never marry again? Did the memory of this lost enchantment hold his heart a prisoner?

She read Josh his story, but she wasn't certain she could have told anyone what it was about. Then she tucked him in and bent over to kiss his tousled hair.

The thunder had died down, but he clung to her. 'Don't go away,' he said.

'But you can't very well go to sleep with me sitting here watching you.'

'No,' he admitted reluctantly, 'but I'll feel better if you stay upstairs.'

'Where I'm handy if you need me?'

Josh nodded. 'You can sleep in Daddy's room,' he offered helpfully. 'He won't mind.'

Jill started to shake her head, then she decided that the matter really wasn't important enough to squabble about. If her staying nearby was all it took to make Josh contented and sleepy, what harm could it do? 'All right. I'll stay up here for a few minutes, until you've gone off to sleep again. Then I'll be right downstairs in the great room.'

Josh didn't look as if he fully approved of that plan, but Jill made her escape while he was yawning and couldn't protest.

'I'll just bet Daddy wouldn't mind me sleeping in his room,' she muttered. She picked up a sort of knitted comforter from the foot of the bed and settled herself into the armchair in the corner of Scott's bedroom. 'But I think Daddy might have had a few extra ideas.'

She curled up in the small chair and closed her eyes, cradling her cheek against the soft plush upholstery.

The brush of the fabric against her skin reminded her of Scott's touch. The memory of the way he had stroked her temple with a gentle fingertip, the way his palm had lain warmly against her breast, combined to recreate that shrieking demand deep inside her that had nearly been her undoing earlier.

And you can stop thinking about that right now, she reminded herself. Think about something else—your multiplication tables, that should do the trick—and in a little while you can go back to the couch and get some sleep.

It should only take a few minutes, she told herself. Josh was flat-out tired, and in less than a quarter of an hour he should be safely in dreamland——

'And I shall be in traction,' she mused as she squirmed in the chair, trying to find a comfortable position. 'For a chair that looks attractive, this thing is an invention of the devil!'

She twisted herself around once more and said, 'The hell with it.' What sense was there in mangling her body when less than five feet away was a wonderful bed? She'd lie down for just a minute. There was nothing personal about it, after all, she told herself. It was no different from sleeping in a hotel bed which some stranger had occupied the night before.

But it was very different. For one thing, she realised as soon as she put her head down, the pillow smelled like him. It was a clean scent, a combination of tangy aftershave and soap and something else that was indefinable but that she thought she would recognise if she smelled it in Tanzania—something that was only Scott.

It was only then that she truly admitted that she had never left the memory of him behind, that he had stayed with her through all the years, and that he was the reason that the Gareths of the world had never appealed to her. For what could she find attractive about a self-proclaimed Greek god like Gareth when she could have someone like Scott instead?

But could she have him? Not likely, she reminded herself. And not for long. Even if they were to want more than just a brief affair, all the obstacles that had separated them eight years ago were still just as strongly in place as on the day they had parted, in the tiny sitting-room of her sorority house.

And then there were the other things that hadn't lain between them all those years ago, but which were like concrete walls holding them now in cold and separate cells. Scott's memory of Maria, for one, and the very real reminder of her that at this moment was drifting off to sleep in the next room.

I should have been Josh's mother, she thought. If only Scott had shown some sense, and not insisted on coming here.

But instead, she reminded herself, he had married Maria. That fact alone should tell her all she needed to know—that what he had felt for her had never been love, only a physical attraction. It had been an elemental hunger that had sprung to life again tonight with near-disastrous results.

But it was not love. If it had been, Scott could never have suggested that they simply enjoy the few days that were given to them to be together. If it had been love he felt for her, a few-days-long affair could not satisfy him.

As it could not satisfy her. Her body had been screaming for his lovemaking tonight, and yet she had turned away from him, almost instinctively, because deep inside her she knew it was not enough. She had known that she could not be content with a physical relationship, and she had also known that anything more was impossible.

God help me, she thought. I shall love him till I die, and tonight I turned my back on the only way I had to tell him that. No matter how much it hurt later, it would have been worth it. Perhaps we never really had a chance, but now it's certainly too late.

She closed her eyes and breathed in the scent from his pillow. She felt drained and depressed and half sick, and she knew she should go back downstairs. But it could do no harm, she thought wearily, to lie here for a little bit, until Josh went to sleep. She was so very tired, from two nearly sleepless nights herself. Now that the storm was fading in the distance, perhaps she could rest.

She didn't hear the Cadillac in the still small hours of the night. She didn't hear the back door open, or the footsteps on the stairs, or the weary sigh he released as he stood at the foot of the bed and looked down at her for a full minute.

Then he sat down on the edge of the mattress. 'Jill,' he said softly. His hand brushed the black hair back from her face.

She was dreaming that he had come to her in the depths of the night to tell her that he loved her, and for an instant when she opened her eyes she didn't know if what she saw was real or only a bit of a dream as fragile as tissue-paper. But she knew, even when she was only half awake, that she loved him; she had always loved him, and she would always love him. That alone was what mattered just now. Nothing else had any reality, not the memory of Maria, or the harsh truth of their different ways of life, or the question of whether Scott had ever felt anything more for her than mere desire.

She smiled up at him, a slow and inviting smile, and lifted a hand to stroke his cheek. He needed a shave, and that was what first made her believe that this was really happening, that it was not just a bit of her dream. For the briefest fraction of an instant, she wanted to pull back from this dangerous reality, to turn her face into the pillow and pretend that he wasn't there. Then he leaned over her to brush her lips with his, and she knew that it made no difference to her what tomorrow would hold. For tonight, she told herself, he was mine. There will be no ghosts between us, no concrete walls. And when the barricades are there again in the first light of morning, then I shall still have tonight, to hold to my heart for always.

It was a very soft, very tender kiss, but it ignited a fire-storm that raced along every nerve in Jill's body. She gasped and pulled him down to her, meeting his rising passion with a frantic desire of her own, an aching need to make herself a part of him. There seemed to be no time to waste on gentle caresses, on soft touches and tender embraces. Instead, it was as if every instant since that first afternoon, when she had stepped out of the van and met Scott's eyes, had been an orchestrated prelude to this symphony of love. Each caress, each touch, of the last two days had been only a minor chord, but the effect now was of an explosion of sound, of perfect harmony between two minds, two bodies, two human beings who had waited so very long that they could bear to wait no longer.

When he pulled away, Jill whimpered in frustration and tried to drag him back down to her. Scott laughed, breathlessly, and whispered, 'Take it easy, darling, I'm not going anywhere. I've got just enough presence of mind left to know that making love is a lot more fun without clothes in the way.'

That seemed to make sense, so she clutched the front of his shirt with both hands and ripped.

He shrugged out of the tattered remains and reached for the snap of her jeans. 'It would have been thoughtful of you to undress before you got into bed, Jill.'

'You seem to be doing very well at it,' she said hazily. 'Lots of practice?'

He grinned down at her. 'Beginner's luck,' he whispered huskily. Her bra joined the pile of discards on the floor, and as he bent his head to nibble at her breast, she moaned and drew him down to her. The moment of levity and laughter was past, and the fire between them built to a raging inferno that threatened to consume them alive with its splendour, and then instead deposited them softly back to earth as if all that was left of them was ashes.

When, long minutes later, she could finally begin to breathe again, Jill turned to stare at Scott's face so close beside hers on the pillow. His every muscle was relaxed. All the tension was gone from him, and though his hand still curved around her breast, it was a light, almost accidental touch. She felt betrayed, and almost angry that after what they had shared, he could so easily go to sleep——

'What's wrong?' he asked softly. He opened his eyes, then, and she stared into the brown depths, in the fading darkness, and sighed.

'Nothing.'

He rose up on one elbow and looked down at her. 'What is it, Jill?'

She licked her lips, nervously, and his fingertip lifted to her face as if he intended to trace the damp line left by her tongue.

'Are you sorry?' he whispered. He nibbled at her throat. It was a teasing, tickling sensation rather than a sexual one, and she felt the stirring of regret that something so beautiful could not last forever.

'Not exactly,' she muttered. 'It's just that——' She tried to tell him what had been going through her mind. She felt a little shamefaced at even thinking it, much less putting it into words. You sound like a wanton woman, she told herself.

He heard her out, then smiled and murmured, very softly, 'Who says it's over?'

'But it's almost morning, Scott.' Jill could see the eastern sky beginning to turn pink.

'It's almost dawn,' he countered. 'It's a whole different thing this time of year.' He moved just a little, turning her on to her back, and began to play with her nipple. The wetness of his tongue and the cool of the morning air combined to form a sensation that sent thrills of pleasure to the core of her.

She moaned and stroked his hair with unsteady fingers, and he raised his head to give her a mischievous smile. 'You said you didn't want to be in a hurry,' he reminded her. Then he started in earnest to stir every square inch of her to white heat, with relentless thoroughness.

It was slow, ecstatic torment, and within a few minutes she was clinging to him, pleading, her body demanding satisfaction. Her impatience fuelled his desire, and when his self-control ultimately snapped, she was fiercely glad for an instant, until her own sense of reason was swallowed up in the chaos that raged between them, and she could not think at all.

She didn't think she had slept, merely closed her eyes

to enjoy lying in the comforting circle of his arms. But
when she roused, full sunlight was streaming through
the wide windows. Her first thought was a sleepy
observation on the beauty of the day, and then her
eyes snapped wide. 'Good God, what time is it?'

'Not all that late,' said Scott, without stirring.
'About half past six. Why?'

I'm supposed to be reporting for work this very
minute, she was thinking. Joe Niemann is going to kill
me.

She slid out of Scott's arms and scrambled from the
big bed. The floor was strewn with clothes, and she
had a hard time assembling the ones that were hers.

'Why are you in such a hurry?' asked Scott. He sat
on the side of the bed, watching with a mixture of
puzzlement and appreciation, as she struggled into
her jeans.

'Because in less than half an hour I'm supposed to
be out in that field, with make-up and clothes and
ready to start shooting, that's why!'

'After all that rain?' he scoffed. 'That cornfield
probably looks like a lake this morning.'

Jill pulled the zipper of her jeans half-way up and
the tab came off in her hand. She swore and dropped
it in her pocket. 'Perhaps it is,' she said. 'But I'm not
the one who calls off shooting. And unless the director
cancels, we work, even if that means we only sit in the
van and wait.'

'All right, I get the picture. But I was out in that
storm last night, and I know you won't be shooting
today. Believe me, that wasn't just a gentle little
shower.'

She stopped abruptly. 'I didn't even ask you how
bad the mess was at the store, did I?'

Scott grinned. 'That's all right,' he drawled. 'The

subject you chose instead didn't hurt my feelings any.'

The appreciative gleam in his eyes brought a warm flush to her face.

He patted the edge of the bed suggestively. 'Joe Niemann isn't going to make you sit out there all day and wait for the mud to dry out, Jill. I'm betting he tells you to take the day off instead.'

She shook her head. 'It's still not up to me. I have to report for work.' By holding her breath and sucking in her stomach, she managed to pull the zipper up without the tab. 'For all I know, Joe's got something else in mind for today.'

'So do I,' he murmured, and his gaze wandered over her trim figure. 'Why don't you call him, and then come back to bed?'

She turned to stare at him. 'You can't be serious! Josh may pop his head in at the door any minute.'

'Does the idea bother you so much?'

She stopped with her blouse half over her head, then pulled it deliberately into place. 'As a matter of fact, it does. Doesn't it trouble you? Or does Josh see this sort of thing so regularly that it doesn't disturb him any more?'

His eyes darkened at the jab, and Jill wished she hadn't let her tongue get out of control.

'I'm surprised, if that's what you think, that you didn't scream and run the moment I touched you,' he said curtly.

Perhaps I should have, she thought wearily. As beautiful as the night had been, cold reality was setting in. Josh, and her job, and all the logical things that she had forgotten last night, were once more raising their demanding voices.

'I was half asleep when you came in,' she said quietly. 'I only knew what I wanted right then, not what was the wise and intelligent thing to do.'

'And what would that have been? To walk out?'

'Probably. At least it would have avoided this problem, wouldn't it?' She ran her hands through her hair. It resembled an abandoned bird's nest when she was finished. Thank heaven there was a brush in her handbag downstairs. 'Scott, really, I just don't have time to argue about it now.'

He came across the room to her. The watchful strain hadn't gone out of his eyes, but his voice was gentle. 'I'm sorry, Jill,' he said. 'I guess I'm not being very wise and intelligent at the moment either, am I? I, too, only know what I want.' He cupped her face in both hands and turned it up to his, and kissed her with a restrained passion that made her ache. 'We've got just these precious few days—let's not waste them in quarrelling over things that don't matter.'

Jill nodded unhappily. She looked back at him from the doorway. He was standing very still in the centre of the room, heedless of his state of undress, watching her with a hunger that nearly made her throw common sense to the winds and run back to him. But she ran down the stairs instead.

Brilliant light cascaded through the high clerestory windows in the great room, and she stopped in the doorway for a long instant, astounded at the enormous change such a little thing as sunlight made. The dimness that had so irritated her was gone, and the colours of fabric and wood and stone seemed to sparkle invitingly.

It's a beautiful room, she thought. How could I have ever thought the shadows were ominous?

But there was certainly no time to think about things like that! She seized her handbag and let herself out of the front door into the quiet morning.

Damn, she thought. My car's still in Cassie's garage!

And the door was locked. Well, she thought, I don't have time to waste on explanations, that's certain. I'll just have to walk back to the motel now and pick up the car some other time.

The rented van was parked beside the Journey's End, not under the canopy where they had gathered each morning. She released a huge sigh of relief. Perhaps she wasn't as late as she had thought. If she could just get to her room and pick up her tote bag——

'Well, if it isn't our favourite perpetually missing person!' a male voice called from the little restaurant off the corner of the main lobby. 'Come on in and have a cup of coffee.'

Gareth. Jill groaned and thought about pretending not to have heard him, but she knew that would only fuel suspicion and talk among the entire crew. He was alone, though, she realised. That was a bit strange; Gareth was never the first one to report in the mornings.

She sank into the seat across from him and signalled the waitress to bring an extra cup. A jolt of caffeine might help, she thought; it certainly couldn't hurt. 'Gareth, you look wonderful, considering what happened yesterday,' she said. Gareth was constitutionally unable to recognise flattery, and besides, it was nearly true; he was sitting very still, as if he felt a bit stiff, but there was no other evidence of his injury.

He studied her over the rim of his cup and said, 'Too bad I can't say the same about you. You look exhausted, Donovan. Tell me, what have you found to do in this town that wears you out so?'

Jill occupied herself with stirring her coffee. 'I think

it's a rather nice little town,' she found herself saying, and was a bit surprised at herself for defending it.

'Of course, being on the edge of nowhere has a few advantages,' sniffed Gareth. 'Personally, I've stored up enough sleep to carry me for a month when I get back to civilisation. There doesn't seem to be anything more useful to do. Have you found something else to occupy yourself, or have you been spending all your time in bed too?'

She ignored the innuendo, but it took an effort. 'Where's the rest of the crew? I thought Joe said he wanted an early start today.'

'He got it,' Gareth said. 'He was out to check that field at the crack of dawn, and now he's figuring out what to do next. I'm going back to bed while he decides.'

'It's too wet to shoot?' Scott was right, she thought, with the tiniest twinge of sadness. I could have stayed with him after all.

Then she reminded herself that it really wouldn't have made any difference. The magical night is over, she thought, and first thing this morning we crashed into harsh reality. It isn't going to be easy to sort this out.

Let's not waste these precious few days, Scott had said. They had shared a wonderful time together, that was all. This was a crossroads of their lives, a few brief days to be snatched and enjoyed. And you'd better make up your mind to that, Jill, she told herself with determination. If you try to dissect the magic, you'll only destroy the beauty of the days we still can have. So you're just going to enjoy it, and not worry about tomorrow.

For the first time, she felt glad that the weather had not co-operated with Joe Niemann's schedule. Every

extra day with Scott would be another glowing ember
to add to a precious, hidden fire banked deep inside
her, a fire that had warmed her once and that would
have to keep her warm for always.

Even more astounding, she realised as she sipped
her coffee, was that she actually felt glad this morning
that the magazine cover had been cancelled. This
project can drag out as long as Joe Niemann's patience
and North Star's budget will allow, she thought
dreamily, and I won't care. Of course I'll be glad to go
back to New York and into the mainstream. That's
my life. But if that day is a couple of weeks away, who
cares?

Joe Niemann pulled a chair out from the table and
sat down heavily. He rubbed a hand wearily across his
jaw and said, 'You look like hell, Donovan.'

'And a bright good morning to you too, Joe,' Jill
returned sweetly.

'And you're getting freckles.'

Gareth leaned across the table to inspect her nose,
and nodded. He looked delighted.

Jill would have liked to stab him with her butter
knife. 'What do you expect, when you put me out in a
cornfield day after day?'

'No more cornfields,' said Joe.

'Well, that's certainly a relief,' Gareth murmured.

Jill stared at the director for a long moment. 'What
do you mean, no more cornfields?' she asked warily.
'So what if it got a little wet—it'll dry up, won't it?'

'In a week, maybe,' said Joe. 'And it isn't just the
rain. The high winds last night took that corn and laid
it down flat in the water. It looks like a three-day-old
battlefield out there.'

She was a little dazed. Of course, she thought,
remembering the rain rattling against the windows

last night. The wind had been strong, and of course it had caused damage. But surely, in a day or two——

'And since we've been having so much trouble with corn, anyway,' Joe said wearily, 'the company decided that we'd do better with wheatfields in Kansas instead. They're working on finding us a field. Pack your bags—we're leaving this afternoon, just as soon as they call back and tell us exactly where we're going.'

CHAPTER NINE

LEAVE Springhill—and Scott? Jill thought blankly. Now? Today? When she had finally chosen to take the pleasure she could have, instead of longing for the unattainable, how could she now just walk away from what they had shared as if it had never been?

I have to have just a few more days, she thought. I'm not asking for forever, but to have to go now——

'Joe, that's completely ridiculous,' she protested. 'After all the work we've gone to.'

'What's the matter, Donovan?' jibed Gareth. 'Have you already lined up a hot date for the weekend? What do you see in him, anyway?'

She glared at him, and turned to Joe.

'After all the work we've gone to,' he said in a very deliberate tone, 'we have not one single usable photograph, and you know that just as well as I do, Jill.'

'But I thought——'

'You're not paid to think. This week, you're paid to sit on the seat of an all-terrain vehicle and look beautiful. Which part of the United States we put the vehicle in is not your concern.'

Joe's tone wasn't as harsh as his words, but Jill swallowed hard at the rebuke, anyway. He was absolutely right, she told herself. And yet——'When are we leaving?' she asked.

'Whenever my boss calls back to tell us where we're going.'

'Surely you're not expecting everyone to sit in the lobby all day and wait,' Jill said tartly. 'There are

148

things I'd like to do.'

Joe looked at her sharply, and she half expected him to explode. But there was a trace of compassion in his voice. 'I expect it will be mid-afternoon at least before they have anything definite. Report here by three, Jill.' He pushed his chair back and strode out of the dining-room.

'That wasn't real bright, Donovan,' Gareth observed.

Jill shrugged, trying to hide the horrified tremors that were shaking her. 'It's a beautiful day. Who wants to spend it sitting inside, waiting for a telephone call?'

'What do you have in mind instead—lining up another job? It's obvious that you'd better start thinking that way, you're certainly losing your edge in the modelling business.'

'And what makes you think that, Gareth?'

'Only superstars throw temper tantrums to the director and get away with it, Donovan, and for your information, you're not in that league.'

'I think Joe understands quite well that this sudden change came as a shock,' she said stiffly. And just why, she asked herself, am I wasting any moment of this precious last day talking to Gareth? I'll have to listen to him all the way to Kansas; why start now? She jumped up.

'Well, you'd better watch your step,' Gareth warned, 'or you'll get the reputation of being hard to handle. And once you're tagged with that——'

'You should know what it's like,' she said sweetly from the doorway, and dashed up to her room for a quick shower.

It *was* a beautiful day, with the air as crisp and clear as if it had been scrubbed by the rain. It somehow made it even more difficult to bear, Jill thought. Farewells should be said at gloomy twilight, or in a dreary drizzle of rain.

Josh and another little boy were riding their bikes in the traffic circle in front of Cassie's house when Jill walked down Clearview Court for the last time. The early sunshine hadn't dried the streets completely yet, and long shadows still lay across the wet lawns. Here and there a robin hopped about over the grass in search of breakfast.

Josh saw her coming, and his bicycle sped wildly down the pavement towards her. He did a daredevil's turn and slid off the bike at her feet, throwing his arms around her in a bear hug and chattering about the unexpected treasure he had found under his pillow that morning. 'And next time I lose a tooth we'll write a note again,' he said excitedly, 'and then I'll get another dollar!'

Jill laughed at the excited cascade of words. And then she remembered that she would probably never again share in Josh's triumphs, his joys and his sorrows, because she was going away.

Half of her—the selfish half—wanted him to be upset that she was leaving. The other half hoped that he wasn't going to miss her, because to know that she had injured him would make leaving even more awful.

She hugged him again, trying with all her strength to make it seem a casual gesture, and sent him back to his friend. Then she rang the doorbell.

Cassie came to the door barefoot and looked Jill up and down with an air of speculation, as if looking for evidence of dissipation. 'I came to pick up the MG,' Jill explained.

Cassie opened the door. 'I reckoned you'd remember it some time.'

That didn't sound promising. 'I didn't want to disturb you earlier, and the garage door was locked.' Jill tried to make a joke of it. 'I thought you trusted everybody in town, Cassie.'

'Trust is one thing,' Cassie said sombrely. 'Idiocy is another.'

Jill thought she probably wasn't talking about garage doors. 'I——'

'For heaven's sake, Jill, can't you be a bit more discreet?' Cassie sounded furious. 'I know I told you that gossip isn't too bad in this town, but you are hot news, and there are people who would love to spread the word.'

'What do you mean?'

Cassie looked at her bleakly. 'The first thing Josh volunteered when he walked in the door this morning was that you'd stayed overnight and slept in his daddy's bed, that's what I mean. He seemed rather pleased at the idea, and it was quite a balancing act to convince him that he shouldn't announce it, without destroying his innocence.'

'Oh.' Jill tried to conceal her shock with a laugh. 'Did he also tell you that Scott spent the night at the store dealing with damage from the storm?' It was far from the whole truth, but surely, under the circumstances, she could be forgiven for the omission, she told herself.

'No. Did he?'

Jill said crisply, 'If you're worried about keeping Scott safe for yourself, let me assure you——'

'Oh, for heaven's sake!' Cassie looked disgusted. 'I told you yesterday that Scott and I are friends. There's nothing romantic between us, and there never could be. If you can't even tell your friends from your enemies, Jill——'

Jill stared at her for a long moment. There was rage in Cassie's eyes, but there was hurt as well. Jill held out a hand to her and she said softly, 'I'm sorry I didn't trust you, Cassie.'

'The way you've been carrying on—well, it looks to

me as if Scott's lost any common sense he ever had where you're concerned, and I'm darned if I'm going to see Josh hurt because of it.'

And that, Jill thought, summed the whole problem up quite neatly. It's just as well, she thought, that I'm leaving today, before we're all drawn further into this impossible mess.

She backed the car out into the traffic circle and waved at Josh. She had no intention of actually saying goodbye to him—it would be better to treat the whole thing casually, she thought. People come and go every day, and to make a production out of the farewells would only encourage him to be upset.

But when she had gone just a few feet down the street, she put on the brakes, got out of the car, and walked back to him. She couldn't bear to go away without saying goodbye.

There was a sort of stoicism in his face when she told Josh that she was leaving. He nodded, and he wouldn't quite look her directly in the eyes. That evasion from this direct and trusting child hurt her, and she found herself telling him that he could visit her in New York some day. Then she wanted to bite her tongue off for making foolish promises, promises that would probably never come to anything.

He just nodded again. When she drove away, he was riding his bike once more, making slow and aimless circles on the concrete. The same sort of slow and aimless circles that Jill was making in her mind.

She tracked Scott down in the nuts-and-bolts aisle at the hardware store, helping a customer to find the right size fastener. He looked up from the bins of parts and gave her a smile that would have melted her into a gluey puddle on the floor if she hadn't had other things on her mind at the moment. 'I told you Joe wouldn't make you work today,' he murmured, and turned back to his customer.

'I have to talk to you,' Jill said desperately, in a tone that allowed no argument.

'I'll be with you in five minutes, Jill,' he said, but it was closer to a quarter of an hour before the satisfied customer went off with a small paper bag containing fifteen cents' worth of hardware.

Jill was pacing the floor by then. That can't possibly be cost-effective, she was thinking. He's the owner of the place, after all, and his time must be far too valuable to waste it on petty details like a few cents' worth of nuts and bolts.

You couldn't care less about the business, Jill, she told herself. Not today, at any rate. It's just that today, I want his every minute for myself.

Scott came up behind her quietly, and his fingers brushed over her still-damp hair. 'Were you so anxious to get back to me?' he murmured. 'That's very flattering, my dear.'

There was nothing in his touch or his words that was intimate or embarrassing, and yet the very huskiness of his voice sent sensual shivers through every cell of Jill's body. She turned to look up at him and laid a slim hand pleadingly on his chest. She could feel his heartbeat beneath the thin shirt.

A customer said, 'Where are the thumb tacks, Scott?'

'Three aisles over,' Scott said, pointing. 'How are you today, George?'

George admitted, after a little consideration, that he was fine. It was also obvious that he was curious as to why Scott Richards was standing in the middle of aisle with a woman practically in his arms.

This is impossible, Jill thought. We can't talk here.

'Come with me, Scott,' she said suddenly. 'Let's drive up to that little lake and spend the day——'

He was shaking his head. 'Can't,' he said briefly. 'I have half my people working on drying out stock, so I'm short-handed on the floor. I can't just walk out, no matter how much I'd like to.'

That's the end of it, then, she thought helplessly. We'll have to say goodbye here, with people around.

And it's probably just as well not to have it dragged out, she decided. Don't delay it, Jill, she ordered herself. Tell him. Be bright and cheerful and casual—it's not a disaster, after all; you've both always known that you would be leaving. You just didn't expect it to be today, that's all.

Scott brushed a thumb across her lips. 'Shall we get a babysitter tonight? If you like Sapphire Lake, we could go up there. I've got a cabin right on the shore. We'll have a picnic dinner on the beach, and then I'll take you into my cabin and show you my collection of driftwood.' His voice was a sensual caress.

If he has a collection of driftwood, Jill thought, I'll eat it. It sounds more like the proverbial etchings to me.

Then she remembered that she couldn't go anywhere tonight, except to Kansas. She shook her head.

'What's wrong, Jill?' His voice was suddenly stern. 'Last night——'

'Last night should never have happened,' she said morosely.

'What the hell are you talking about?'

'You were right, Scott. About the storm. The field's not only too wet to use, it's ruined. We're leaving this afternoon.'

There was dead silence for a long moment. His hand seemed to have frozen, and it weighed heavily against the nape of her neck.

She looked up at him through her long lashes. His face was all tense angles and harsh shadows, but his voice was surprisingly gentle as he said, 'And that's it, then? Is this the way it ends, Jill?'

Of course it is, she thought. What other possibilities are there, my love? You said last night that these few days were all we could expect. We just didn't think it would be so very short, that's all.

'I have to go, Scott.' She wanted it to sound firm, matter-of-fact. Instead, her voice trembled.

His hands moved jerkily to rest on her shoulders. 'You could stay a few days, surely.' His voice was unsteady. 'You said the magazine cover had been cancelled.'

'It has,' Jill said blankly. Then she realised what he meant. 'I didn't mean I'm going back to New York today, I wish I were. But Joe's not giving up on this campaign just yet.'

'I see.' It was curt.

Why can't he understand that I don't have any choice? she thought. 'It is my job, after all,' she pointed out. 'I can't just walk out on it. If I do, I'll be blacklisted, and I'll never work again.'

'Would that be the end of the world, Jill?'

'Of course it would! My job is important to me!'

'Sometimes this week it has seemed to me that you don't like it all that well, that you're holding on out of habit, rather than any real drive to continue.'

'I don't happen to enjoy working in cornfields, no!' Jill snapped. 'That doesn't mean I don't like modelling at all. How would you know what it's like to work in civilisation?'

Scott's hands slipped heavily from her shoulders, and he turned away as if he didn't want to look at her any more.

She bit her lip, and went on in a calmer tone. 'Scott, we could have this one last day. You said yourself that we shouldn't waste time arguing about stupid things. We could have a few more hours, at least.'

'What are you suggesting, Jill? That we have one more romp in bed, before I kiss you goodbye and send you off to wherever the hell you're going? No, thanks. It seems to me that last night was quite unforgettable enough—too much so, for my taste.'

She turned shock-white at the harshness of his tone.

'You're right, you know,' he said heavily. 'Last night should never have happened.'

'I'm sorry that you found me such a nuisance! I suppose I should thank you for hiding your feelings so well when you came in and found me in your bed.'

'Oh, for God's sake, Jill, you know better than to suggest any such thing. It's just that I want more than that!'

'Really? And what do you have in mind?'

For a long moment she thought he hadn't heard her at all. Then he turned slowly to face her, and she saw the dullness in his eyes and heard it in his voice as he said, 'I want you to marry me, Jill.'

For one splintered second she thought she heard bells chiming. That means he must still love me, she was thinking. I'm not just a few days' entertainment.

Then he cupped her face in his hands and said huskily, 'Stay here with me, Jill. We can be happy together, you know we can.'

The sparkling chime of the bells turned into warning buzzers in her brain, and she snapped, 'Stay here? We're right back where we started, aren't we, Scott? Am I supposed to be flattered that you want me to warm your bed every night?'

'If a warm body in my bed was all I wanted,' he said

brutally, 'I'd have been married again four years ago.'

'I suppose I should be touched that you think I'm capable of filling Maria's place?'

'Nobody is expecting you to take Maria's place, Jill.' His voice was hard.

It hurt as badly as if he had slapped her. 'I'm honoured by the compliment you've paid me, Scott,' she said sarcastically, 'but you can't seriously think I would consider staying here. I can't model here. I can't even go back to my first career choice and work in an art museum here! What is there in this town for me?'

There was a long silence. Then he said quietly, 'I'm here. But I suppose it's foolish of me to think that might be enough, isn't it, Jill?'

'You're darned right it's foolish. What do you expect me to do with myself while you're at work, Scott? I can't even take a picture of your son that's good enough to suit you.'

'I didn't say the pictures weren't good, exactly,' he began.

'What do you suggest I do with my time? Be the little woman? Do needlepoint and dream up new ways to make spaghetti sauce?'

'Of course I'm not saying that you should sit at home and wait for me. There are hundreds of things you could do.'

'I could have babies, of course,' she said sarcastically. 'Is that what you had in mind? I suppose half a dozen would be enough to meet your ideas of proper conduct for a wife!'

His eyes were fierce. 'Would it be so awful for you, Jill, if I asked you to carry my child?'

She had a sudden vision of what it would be like to snuggle a baby—his baby—to her breast. It was so real that she could actually feel the warm, damp weight in

her arms, and see a pair of brown eyes—Scott's
eyes—looking up at her with trust.

Don't be foolish, she told herself. You've never
wanted to have a child.

Not until you got to know Josh, she thought. And
then you began to think it might not be such a bad idea.

That's quite enough of that sort of ridiculous
thinking, she reminded herself.

Scott went on quietly, 'I think there's one hell of a lot
more to you than the frozen front you want everyone to
see, Jill. I've watched you with my son. You weren't
pretending. I happen to believe that you were more real
with him than you've been in years, except for last night,
in my bed.'

'Stop it, Scott! This isn't fair.'

'Do you really want to end your life alone, Jill? A cold
and lonely woman, without a single human being who
shares your blood, your dreams, your heritage?'

No, she thought. But neither do I want to end my life
here in this town, bored and resentful and regretting my
lost opportunities. That sort of anger would poison us,
no matter how much love we had for each other.

And Scott, she reminded herself, had not exactly said
that he loved her. 'Why did you ask me to marry you,
Scott?' she asked.

He rubbed a hand over the back of his neck. 'Because
I think we're meant to be together.'

'If you're so certain of that,' she challenged, 'why
don't you come back to New York with me, instead of
insisting that I move here? Your father is gone, you don't
have to stay in Springhill. Other people can sell bolts
just as well as you can. I've got connections with the
advertising agencies, Scott. You're good, and you could
go to work for any of them.'

'And lose myself in the clamour of Madison Avenue?

No, Jill.'

'But that's the same sacrifice you're asking of me—to lose myself in the dead silence of Springhill!'

'It's not the same thing.' Scott rubbed his temples as if his head hurt. 'You're missing the point, Jill. I never was the kind of person who fits into an agency, the pressure of Madison Avenue would crush me. And now I've been my own boss for too long; I can't go back to taking orders. I can't be another Joe Niemann, and it would stifle me to try.'

'Don't you think what you're asking would stifle me, Scott?'

'But you can't be a model forever, my dear.' His voice had a note of gentle persuasion, under the firmness. 'You'll have to find something else to do, one day, some other way to use your creative energy.'

'But even if you're right about that, which I am not admitting, what I do will still be in New York,' she pointed out.

'It doesn't have to be, Jill.'

'You're very certain of that.'

'Yes, I am certain. And all I'm asking is that you make that change a little earlier than you might otherwise.'

'As if everything you're asking me to give up isn't important at all, compared with the wonderful prize I'll have in getting you! You really think you're the greatest thing that could ever happen to a woman, don't you?'

He didn't answer. 'Why is it that you haven't ever married, Jill?'

'I never found time,' she said sullenly.

'I don't believe that. Other models have husbands, even families. I think you've stayed single because you knew, deep down, that you should have married me eight years ago.'

'And made you miss out on Maria?' she scoffed. She

saw the anger flare in his eyes, and something else as well—was it hurt? She felt ashamed of herself for bringing up Maria again—ashamed, and a little afraid of the shadow she had raised.

'And Josh,' Scott reminded her harshly. 'Don't forget about him. If it were only me, Jill, I might follow you, as much as I hate the city. But I've got Josh to consider.' He looked at her, sharply. 'Or are you suggesting that I leave Josh behind too, along with the store? You've said often enough that you aren't the motherly type, and having him around would tie you down.'

She wanted to strike him, then, to hurt him as that accusation had hurt her. 'Of course I wouldn't expect you to give up Josh,' she snapped. 'But children grow up in New York City too, you know!'

'I'm sorry,' he said unsteadily. 'That was uncalled for. My temper got the better of me.' He put out a gentle hand to brush a lock of hair back over her shoulder.

'I wouldn't hurt him,' she muttered.

'Don't you realise that you already have? I know the way you affect me, the way you've always been able to make me toss all logic to the winds. The one thing I never dreamed, Jill, is that my six-year-old would look into those green witch's eyes of yours and fall in love too.'

She remembered the set, tense look on Josh's face that morning. 'I'm sorry,' she said. Her voice was shaking. 'I didn't mean to.'

'I know you didn't. You just can't help it, can you?'

'He'll forget.'

'The same way I've forgotten?' It was rueful. 'I've thrown a lot at you all at once, haven't I? It's no wonder you're upset. But please don't say no, Jill, not till you've really thought about it. Perhaps I was a little hasty in asking you to give your job up altogether, today.'

'A little hasty?' she repeated. 'You sounded like a barbarian dictating terms to the conquered country!'

Scott smiled at that, but the humour didn't reach his eyes. 'Please, Jill, think about what I've asked. Go, if you have to, but——'

She could feel herself wavering under the husky charm of his voice. She was almost swaying on her feet from exhaustion and nerves and desire and confusion—a deadly brew that threatened to send her sobbing into his arms for comfort. But her brain could still command a tiny bit of logic, and it told her that what Scott offered would be a short-lived comfort. And what would follow? Feelings of anger? Hurt? Betrayal? She loved him too much to allow that to happen, she told herself. Better to love him and never have him than to marry him and end up hating him for it.

She shook her head stubbornly. 'No,' she said. 'There's nothing to think about. It's impossible, Scott. We're too different. Our lives won't cross again.'

His jaw set firmly, and she braced herself for yet another outburst. But it didn't come. He looked down into her eyes for a long moment, then he sighed. 'That's all there is to say, then.'

Jill nodded wearily.

He cupped her face in his hand, his palm warm against her cheek, and bent his head till his lips met hers, long and softly. She closed her eyes and drank in the bittersweet pleasure of their farewell kiss.

'Mr Richards? They've been calling you on the intercom. There's a telephone call for you.'

Jill struggled back to sanity slowly, her eyelids fluttering. Scott didn't move for a long moment; he was still staring down at her. She turned her head and saw the young man who had waited on her the day she had first come into the hardware store to buy a chamois. He was staring.

'Sorry,' Scott said. 'I was preoccupied.'

'I should say,' the young man muttered.

Scott ignored him. 'Sorry I can't see you to your car, Jill.' He turned on his heel and walked away.

Silently, she stood in the nuts-and-bolts aisle and watched him go out of her life.

She knew she should take the car back to the dealer and turn it in, then go to the model and pack her things and get ready to leave. But instead she found herself on the empty highway north of the little town, driving aimlessly, unwilling to give up the bit of freedom that the little MG represented. As long as she had it, she could pretend that she was independent. She couldn't bear to go back to the motel just now and sit with Gareth and Danny and the others and wait.

If only Scott didn't have to be so stubborn, she thought. He was using Josh for an excuse, that was certain. There was no real reason why he couldn't come to New York.

She found herself at the turnoff that led to Sapphire Lake. She took the winding country road without hesitation, hoping to find again the peace she had felt that first day as she sat beside the crystal water.

I should be furious with Scott, she told herself. Furious at the very idea of his wanting me to give up everything that's important to me and make myself into an adoring wife, a nonentity of a woman who's a mere reflection of him, just as he wanted me to do eight years ago!

But he hadn't, exactly, she realised, as she thought about it. Eight years ago, yes, he had assumed that she would be content to be his wife. But today—'Some day you'll have to find some other way to use your creative energy,' he had said. That certainly didn't imply that he expected her to do nothing but make beds and wash socks——

Whoa! she told herself. Whatever he had said, the fact remained that there were few options for her in this town. And that brought her directly back to his stuborn-ness, for there were a million opportunities for Scott in New York, if only he would bring himself to see them. And opportunities for Josh, as well.

She wondered what Josh would think about the city. There were so many things to do—the zoo, the museums, the Statue of Liberty, the Empire State Building. He was a little young to enjoy Broadway, perhaps, but that would come soon enough. Of course, living in her small apartment wouldn't be quite the same as he was used to—the sheer space to spread his belongings out, and the quiet street where he could ride his bike with his friends.

Well, they'd have to get a bigger place, that was all, she thought. The bike she couldn't do much about, but he'd soon make new friends, unless, of course, he was as stubborn as his father, and refused to accept the challenge of a change.

And what about you? she thought. Aren't you being stubborn too? Scott's doing what he thinks is best for his child, but you're just being selfish, wanting to take Josh away from everything he's ever known in his short life. And as for refusing to accept the challenge of a change, what about you?

That's different, she told herself.

She walked down the beach to the fallen tree. Which cabin was Scott's? she wondered, and tried not to think about what tonight might have held—a moonlit picnic, and a walk hand in hand on the beach, and then a retreat to the solitude of that private cabin.

Stop thinking about that, she told herself. It's all over. You won't be seeing him again.

But hadn't he said something about how she had always been able to make him forget logic and follow her?

She turned that over in her mind. Had it only been words? Eight years ago Scott had ignored what she had wanted, and he had come back to Springhill. And yet, now that his father was dead, now that he was free——

'I can persuade him,' she told herself. 'He does care about me, and when he understands that I really can't live here, he'll change his mind and come to New York. And then we can be happy together, Scott and Josh and me.'

It was nearly two o'clock. With a sudden lightness in her heart, and a hope for the future stronger than anything she had felt in years, Jill jumped down from the fallen tree and turned the MG back towards town.

CHAPTER TEN

IT WAS like giving up her right arm when she gave the keys to the MG back to the man at the garage. It was funny, when she didn't own a car, how quickly she had become used to the freedom it represented. Of course, she told herself, in Manhattan a car didn't mean quite the same freedom as it did in Springhill; it would be a nuisance and an extra expense. She could get around the city by bus and taxi far faster than she could walk to a garage, retrieve a car, and drive anywhere. In Manhattan, she thought, just finding a place to park could be a full-time job.

But perhaps when they got to Kansas she would rent a car again. At least then she could explore in the hours when she didn't have to work. She wouldn't have to be dependent on the van, and they might not be so fortunate there as they had been in Springhill, where at least there was a shopping district within walking distance.

You're beginning to sound like the Springhill Chamber of Commerce, she thought drily. That reminded her of Scott. It was one more thing he would miss in New York, the involvement in community affairs.

But there will be other things to compensate, she told herself. He'll have no trouble staying busy.

The man walked around the car and checked the mileage. 'Everything looks fine. Can we give you a ride somewhere, Miss Donovan?'

Jill was stunned. She couldn't imagine the big car-rental agencies worrying about how she would get

165

home! 'I'm going back to the motel. But it's only a few
blocks.'

He turned and called to a young man in a grease-
marked uniform. 'Jim, take Miss Donovan back to the
Journey's End, please.' He tossed the keys to the MG
over the counter.

'Thanks,' Jill said uncertainly. 'What do I owe you?'

The man gave her a conspiratorial smile and tore the
rental agreement papers firmly across the middle. 'Not
enough to bother with the paperwork,' he said. 'Besides,
you people have been good for the town. We'll just
consider it a little favour.'

Jill was so startled that she hadn't recovered her voice
when the young mechanic ushered her out to the MG.

'We're sorry to see you all go,' he volunteered over the
roar of the engine. 'You've been the biggest excitement
around here all summer.'

The funny thing, Jill thought, was that he really
believed he was paying the crew a compliment! 'If it's so
dull,' she said, 'why do you stay in Springhill?'

He grinned. 'I like it here,' he said. 'And as for dull, I
came from a really small town.'

'Smaller than this?' She knew she sounded horrified.

'Much. Springhill's a city in comparison. Besides, my
girl's here,' he added, matter-of-factly, as if that
explained everything.

And perhaps it did, Jill thought.

The MG screeched to a halt under the motel's
canopy. 'This all right, miss?'

'Fine. Thank you. I really appreciate the ride.'

He touched his cap in an old-world, courtly gesture.
'We try to provide service.' The car sped away.

The van was in a corner of the car park, and two of the
crew members were tying down the all-terrain vehicles
on the trailer, making certain they could be safely hauled

across two states. They hadn't been able to locate another trailer, so they were still using the faulty one. Jill shivered and hurried inside. If they had trouble with that ramp again, she didn't want to be anywhere within range.

The door of Gareth's room was closed. She wondered idly if he was still napping. Joe Niemann's door was open; his suitcase was already packed and standing by the bed. Across the hall, Danny's door was open as well. He was bent over the desk, tinkering with a piece of equipment.

Jill tapped on the door and he looked up briefly. 'Hi, Jill. Come on in.'

She shook her head. 'I can't, I haven't packed yet.'

'There's no hurry. The agency hasn't called Joe back yet.' He didn't look up from the open back of the camera.

'Then I'll come in for a minute.' She sat down cross-legged on the foot of the bed. 'Doesn't it take a lot of nerve to tear into a camera like that?'

He shrugged and reached for a tiny screwdriver. 'Don't have much choice sometimes. I wouldn't have been surprised if you hadn't turned up at all.'

'Why?' She was honestly startled.

'I have the impression this week that some other things in your life are more important to you.'

'What things?' Jill asked icily.

He turned to face her. 'Got a guilty conscience, Jill? I meant things like staying up till all hours and eating what you liked, that's all. You've got dark circles under your eyes and you've gained at least two pounds. Those are sure signs that a model's going to bail out.'

'Well, your sure signs took a detour this time, Danny. I've had an unusual week, but that doesn't mean I'm quitting. I plan to model just as long as I can.'

'And how long do you think that will be?'

It sounded like a casual question, but Jill found herself stumbling for an answer. Just how long was she hoping to go on with her career? she asked herself. Another five years at least. Ten, perhaps, if fate was kind to her and she aged gracefully.

When she didn't answer, Danny turned around again, and his eyes narrowed as he inspected every line of her face. Then he shook his head. 'You're not the model you used to be, Jill. You're getting bored with it all, aren't you?'

'Of course not,' she said tartly. 'It's just this blasted cornfield.'

Danny shook his head. 'I saw you stand in Central Park last August in mink, from eight in the morning till well after dark, without a murmur. And it was a hundred and three degrees.'

'That's different. Any woman would put up with odd conditions if she could drift around Central Park wearing mink.'

'You're avoiding the question, Jill.' He whistled, a tuneless little murmur, as he tightened a screw and tested the camera's reaction. 'You never used to get impatient. That's why we all liked to work with you so well. If it had been up to the camera people alone, you'd have been a superstar. Now——' He shook his head.

'Only superstars can throw tantrums and get away with it,' Gareth had said just this morning. It echoed unpleasantly in Jill's brain. Across the hall, Joe Niemann's telephone rang.

'It's this job, Danny,' she said. 'When I get back to New York——'

'I don't think that's what's wrong. Not entirely. This job may have put the finishing touches on the problem, but it started before you ever got here.'

'So you think Gareth's right? I'm finished as a model?' Her voice was dry.

'No, I don't think you're finished. But you'll have to work harder than ever before to keep your place, and I wonder if you still want it badly enough to do that.'

'Of course I do.' It was sharp enough to end the discussion. Jill uncoiled herself from the bed. 'I'd better get packed. That must be the agency Joe's talking to.'

'Sorry if I offended you, Jill.'

She stopped at the door. He didn't sound sorry, she thought resentfully. And it wasn't any of his business, anyway. But Danny had always been a friend. 'No offence,' she said stiffly.

Joe Niemann's voice stopped her at the door. She could hear only half of the conversation, but it obviously wasn't going well. 'Damn it,' he said, very clearly. '*I'm* the one in charge here. This is my campaign, and I don't understand why——'

He broke off and turned towards the door, and Jill sidestepped out of his line of vision. It wasn't that she exactly felt guilty about what she had heard, she thought; if he didn't want to be overheard he should have closed the door. But there was something about the tone of his voice that made her suspect he would rather not have anyone listening in.

'If you had just given me a decent budget——Is that a direct order?' he asked. 'All right, you've made your point. Yes, I'll be in your office first thing Monday morning. But I don't think I have anything to explain!' The telephone hit the desk with a crash that made Jill wince.

She was half-way down the hall to her room when Joe came out of his. 'You might as well unpack, Donovan,' he called to her. 'We're not going to Kansas.'

Reprieve, she thought, and happiness swelled inside

her till she thought she would burst from it. I can go up to the lake with Scott tonight, she thought, and we can talk it all over.

And what will we solve? she asked herself. What will we change?

Don't be such a pessimist, she ordered herself. Surely, given a little more time, you can make him see how important it is that he comes with you!

She retraced her footsteps. Joe was rubbing his eyes wearily, and she asked, with sudden suspicion, 'So what are we doing instead?'

Danny had come out of his room too. 'Trouble with the boss, Joe? he asked casually.

Joe frowned. 'The whole campaign has been cancelled,' he said bluntly. 'No problem for any of you, you get paid regardless, but I got called on the carpet.'

'What on earth for?' asked Jill. 'The weather isn't your fault.'

'According to my boss, it is. I should have expected something of the sort. The truth probably is that North Star suddenly decided they didn't like the idea so much after all, so someone at the agency is going to have to take the blame. This time, it's me.' He sighed. His eyes were reddened, and he looked suddenly old, and tired.

Jill stared at him and thought, And this is what I've asked Scott to be?

Joe caught the stunned look in her eyes. 'Don't worry about it, Jill,' he said, with an attempt at heartiness. 'Advertising is a chancy game. I've had my neck on the block before, and I've survived. I'll just be out of favour for a while at the agency, till one of the other guys makes a worse mistake.' He rubbed at his eyes again. 'We'll stay here tonight. Might as well; we've already paid for the rooms. We'll leave early in the morning, return the equipment in Chicago, and take the first flight back to

New York. Pass the word, would you, Danny?' He went back into his room and the door closed firmly behind him.

'It isn't that simple, is it, Danny?' whispered Jill. 'That it's just a matter of time till everything is all right, I mean.'

He shook his head. 'I'd say there's a good chance this one might get Joe fired.'

'It wasn't that bad an idea, was it? I never exactly liked it, but——'

'It doesn't have to be a bad idea, Jill,' Danny said sombrely. 'Joe just got caught in the middle. I'd better go tell the guys.'

Jill couldn't bear the thought of her closed-in room, and she had no desire to sit around with the crew and talk in hushed whispers of what was going to happen next. She was still staggered by the emptiness she had seen in Joe Niemann's eyes. He was good at his job, and he had made an honest mistake. Now, he might have to pay for it with his job.

Was this what Scott had meant, when he had said the pressure of Madison Avenue would crush him? And was that what she wanted?

You've been living in a fairy tale, she accused herself, and thinking that Scott's stubbornness was all that was standing in the way of the happy ending.

She got her straw hat and went out into the heat of the afternoon. She walked for a long time, facing the hard truths that she had steadfastly refused to see before.

What if Scott eventually gave in and followed her to New York? She had been so certain that was the answer. But would that make her contented?

'Not if he wasn't happy,' she muttered under her breath. In New York City, in the daily hotbox that was the advertising industry, he might not even remain the

man she loved. He was so much a part of Springhill, and
th town was so much a part of him——

He's a country gentleman, she thought suddenly.
Where the words had come from, she didn't know.
Some half-forgotten bit of Victorian literature, perhaps.
It didn't matter; the phrase described him perfectly. He
fitted into this small town like a bit of a jigsaw puzzle.
But in New York, he would be an anachronism.

Scratch New York, she told herself, and the wonderful
dream of the prince and the princess living happily ever
after . . .

So what other possibilities were there? Could she stay
here? This was the life he had chosen, and he had asked
her to share it with him. But could she give up
everything that mattered to her?

There are no options, she told herself wearily. You go
back to the city where you belong, and he stays here
where he belongs, and that's all there is to do.

And then she knew that there really was such a thing
as heartbreak; she could feel the wrench in her chest,
and the pain slashing out along each nerve till she
wanted to stand still and scream.

Don't be silly, she told herself desperately. You
haven't had lunch. You're just hungry.

She glanced around; she was near the town square,
and there was a tiny restaurant on the corner. She went
in and ordered, then sat staring morosely at her
chocolate milkshake and wondering why she had
ordered it. If she had tried, she couldn't have found
anything further from her ordinary diet.

What was it Danny had said about dark rings under
her eyes, and two extra pounds? Keep this up, my girl,
she thought, and it'll be ten!

Could he be right that she was tired of it all? Was it
possible that Danny could spot such a thing before she

even suspected it herself?

Losing that magazine cover had been a blow, she told herself, but she would recover from that. It would take effort and self-promotion, but she could do it. The question was, did she want to?

She closed her eyes and thought about the endless succession of days when she had first started her modelling career—days of uncertainty and waiting, days of making contacts and hoping that something would turn up and even praying for someone to like her enough to give her that all-important first chance. Was that kind of life to start all over again?

It already has, Donovan, she told herself. Or you wouldn't be out here in the middle of nowhere, doing this campaign. Why didn't you see that before?

Because I was too stubborn to look at it, she thought. Everybody's been telling me that it's time to go gracefully, to do something different with my life. Danny, Gareth, Scott—even Joe Niemann.

All right, she thought. If my modelling career is over, then what am I going to do instead? Stay in Springhill? Be Scott's wife, Josh's stepmother? Lose my identity in theirs? Wasn't that every bit as bad as what she had asked of Scott?

The rush of fear at the idea was mixed with something more, something that was almost pleasure. That's strange, she thought. I know perfectly well I'm going to be miserable unless I can find something else to do, too.

It was a full minute before she realised that she had made her decision.

She stared at the untouched milkshake for thirty seconds longer. Then, very deliberately, she drank it, and decided that it was the best thing she had ever tasted.

She left a tip for the waitress that made the girl starry-

eyed, and cut across the courthouse square. Her heart
was pounding as she went into the small waiting-room at
the front of John Williams' photo studio.

He was standing behind the receptionist's counter.
The young woman at the desk looked up and smiled,
but it was John Williams who said, 'Is there something I
can do for you, Miss Donovan?'

Jill pulled a packet out of her handbag with fingers
that trembled. 'Yes,' she said. 'I'd like you to look at
some pictures.'

She held her breath as she jiggled the knob of the back
door; she was quite certain that Scott had said once that
he left it unlocked for meter readers, but she wouldn't
bet anything on this being her lucky day. And while she
was certain that Cassie had a key, Jill didn't want to go
over there and ask for it. Please, she thought, please let it
be unlocked!

It was, and she let herself into the silent house with a
sigh of relief. It was the work of only a few moments to
unpack the brown paper bag she had been carrying, and
she took a quick survey of the kitchen before she started
her project, whistling under her breath.

'Trying to scare the fidgets away is what you're
doing,' she accused herself. 'Because you've got no idea
what's going to happen when he comes home, and
you've burned every bridge you could think of.'

She told herself stoutly that she had only done what
was necessary. Once her mind was made up, there was
no sense in leaving loose ends dangling, or escape
hatches that might grow to look tempting, she told
herself honestly. And after all, she reminded herself,
Scott *had* asked her to marry him, just this morning.
Surely nothing had changed about that.

But maybe he hadn't meant it, the demon in the back

corner of her brain reminded her. You'd already
announced that you were leaving, and you hadn't left
any doubt about it. Maybe he was certain that you'd
never change your mind, and so he proposed just to
soothe his pride.

Dumb, she told herself. That's the dumbest thing
you've ever thought of, Jill Donovan.

Nevertheless, the doubt didn't quite go away. Just
why had Scott asked her to marry him? He hadn't said
he loved her, only that she had the power to drive him to
make foolish choices. Some foundation for a marriage
that was!

She heard the back door open, and Josh say, 'Can I go
riding bikes with Bobby?'

'Take your sack of cookies to the kitchen first,' Scott
said, but he sounded as if he didn't care.

Josh came around the corner into the kitchen, and his
eyes rounded in wonder. Jill put her finger to her lips,
and he nodded wisely and gave her a silent stranglehold
of a hug.

This, she thought, with a little skip of her heart, from
the child who had said he didn't like smothery hugs!

'What's for dinner?' he whispered. It tickled her ear.

'Spaghetti,' murmured Jill. Josh grinned, dropped the
bag of cookies on the worktop, and went out of the front
door, whistling an off-key little turn.

She heard Scott mutter something that sounded like,
'Heartless little devil,' and braced herself for the
moment when he too came to the kitchen.

Instead, there was a rustle as he moved around the
great room. She heard him say, 'Is Stephanie there?'
and, a moment later, 'This is Scott Richards. Would you
have her call me at home when she gets back, please?'
There was a firm little click as he put the telephone
down.

Jill's jaw tightened. What an idiot you are, Donovan! she told herself fiercely. He thinks you left town barely two hours ago, and he's already calling up a woman.

Anger carried her to the door of the great room, but when she saw him, her fury faded into fear, and concern, and an almost unbearable desire to cry. He had thrown himself down into a big chair. His eyes were closed tightly, as if he didn't want to face the world just now.

'Scott?' she said softly. She moistened her lips, and tried to tell him that she was there to stay. Instead, her voice came out in a half-croak. 'Joe decided to stay one more night.'

Scott came up out of the chair in one motion, so fast that she scarcely saw him move. The naked pain in his face when he saw her was more than she could stand. It sent her reeling back in confusion and despair.

My God, she thought, what have I done? Have I sacrificed everything of importance in my life because he meant more to me, only to find that it was all a mistake?

'Why?' he asked baldly.

'Because the crew's going back to New York instead,' she began uncertainly. 'The whole idea's been cancelled.'

'Why are you here? To what do I owe the honour?' he demanded. 'Haven't you had your fill yet of playing Mommy, playing wife? Or were you doubtful that you'd hooked me securely enough this time to make me come chasing after you, so you came back to make sure?'

'Scott!' It was a horrified whisper. Jill's throat was so tightly constricted that she was amazed she could make any sound at all.

'You just can't stand the idea that I might have learned to live without you in the last eight years, can you, Jill? You couldn't leave me alone.'

'I'm not the one who sought you out this week, Scott.'

Her voice was deadly cold. 'You're the one who wanted to have an affair.'

'Oh, God,' he muttered.

'And as for why I'm here, I guess, if that's what you really think of me, it doesn't much matter any more what I say or what I do. So I might as well tell you the truth. I came here tonight to accept your proposal—to tell you that I'll stay here.'

He looked as if someone had just punched him in the stomach. 'You can't mean that, Jill,' he said unsteadily.

'Why not?' she said bitterly. 'My modelling career is over anyway. I told my agency today that I'm through. So why shouldn't I bury myself here in this god-forsaken nowhere?' She choked on the words. Dammit, she thought, I'm going to start to cry!

He took two steps towards her and then stopped dead and stared as if he had never quite seen her before. 'You shouldn't have done that,' he said. His voice had a sort of crack in it that she had never heard before.

'Why not? In another six months or a year, they would have told me it was over. Why shouldn't I beat them to the punch?'

'Because, dammit, I don't want to be your parachute! You can't run away from things and use me for an excuse, Jill. In a year or two, if you marry me——'

'Don't worry.' Her voice was harsh. 'I don't plan to hold you to your proposal. It's apparent that you didn't really intend me to take it seriously.'

'That's not what I meant. I just don't want you to regret it, and blame me for what you gave up. I was wrong today, Jill, horribly wrong. I let my impatience get in the way of what I knew was right. You've got to go back, don't you see? Because it will only work between us if this is what you want, not because it's the only option you have left.'

She licked her lips, hardly aware that they were so dry that they hurt. 'I've looked at my options, Scott,' she whispered. 'This is the only one I want.'

He shook his head, almost sadly. 'I wish I could really believe that, Jill. But after all this time, and all the things you've said——'

'I love you.'

'Is that going to be enough?'

Jill bit her lip. 'You sound as if you don't even want to try!' Frustration made her voice sharp. 'If you want to back out——'

'Damn it, Jill, it's not that! I want you so badly—I love you so much—that I couldn't bear it if you married me and then were unhappy!'

She shook her head. 'Are you sure the truth doesn't include Stephanie?'

He looked stunned. 'What?'

'You must remember her name,' she said tartly. 'You called her just a little while ago.'

He started to laugh. 'Stephanie is a very good, and very married, real estate broker, Jill.'

She frowned. 'And just what do you need with a real estate bro——' She stopped, and her head began to throb. He can't mean it, she thought helplessly.

'I was going to talk to her about listing my house, and the store, for sale.' It was quiet.

For an instant, Jill's heart danced with gladness. I knew he would do it, she thought. I knew I was more important to him, when it came to the point.

'I can't promise that I shall actually do it,' he warned her.

The world steadied back into place around her. 'I couldn't possibly let you,' she said steadily. 'Because I certainly can't support us, now that I don't have a career any more.' She took a trembling step toward him.

'I'm sorry for everything I said earlier,' he whispered. 'I drove past the car lot garage on the way home, and when I saw that little red MG sitting there, and I knew that you were gone—it felt as if my life had just been blasted into fragments once more.'

As it was when Maria died, she thought.

'To walk in here and find you—and then you said that we had just one more day. I thought once that if I could just have you for a little while, I could let you go again. But I can't, Jill——'

'Scott, would you at least hold me while we talk about it?' she said, and her voice quivered. 'I feel so cold, dissecting our lives this way, and not even touching you——'

For a moment, she thought he would refuse. Then she was in his arms, and he was kissing her eyes, her throat, her mouth, as if there was no appeasing the hunger that possessed him. But finally he raised his head and pulled her over to his big deep chair and down on his lap. He cradled her head against his shoulder and said, with a sigh, 'We'll work it out somehow, Jill.'

'Doing what? Commuting between here and New York? I can't let you sacrifice the store and your house and Springhill.'

'And I can't let you give up your career either.'

'I've already done it. You've got nothing to say about it. Besides, what if I would find a new one?'

'Doing what?' Scott settled her head more comfortably under his chin.

'I know you didn't think much of my pictures of Josh.'

'Did I say that?'

'You did like them?' She twisted around to look up

at him. 'But you didn't want any.'

He sighed. 'I still thought it was possible to get over you, Jill. You'd made it rather plain that evening, if you remember, that you didn't find anything particularly compelling about me.'

'I lied,' she said contentedly, and snuggled her head into his shoulder.

'And I thought it would be easier to forget about you if I didn't have any permanent, physical reminders lying around.'

'Oh.' Jill turned that one over, and smiled up at him. 'Pretty foolish,' she pointed out softly.

'I know. Now what about this new career of yours?'

'At the moment, it's only a job, and a rather poorly paid one at that. John Williams thinks I have a wonderful eye, and he's going to train me. If I like the work, I can buy into the photo studio as a partner, and eventually, when he retires——' She noticed a rising breathlessness, and concluded that Scott might not know where his hands had wandered, but she certainly did.

'I don't know that I'll like it,' she admitted. 'But I want to try, Scott. Did you know John used to work for one of the really big magazines in the East? I couldn't have a better teacher.'

The telephone rang beside his chair, and Scott was laughing as he reached for it. 'All right,' he said. 'I know when I'm out-manoeuvred. I'll tell Stephanie I called because I wanted her to meet my fiancée.'

But the laughter died out of his eyes an instant later, and he handed Jill the telephone. 'For you,' he said curtly. 'A woman. Althea Webb, she said.'

She didn't move off his lap, but she felt him start to withdraw from her. She was a little shaken herself; how had the head of her modelling agency tracked her down here? She hadn't left this number. Joe Niemann was the only possible answer, and yet——

'What is this nonsensical message I found on my desk, Jill?' Althea demanded. 'Have you gone into a great depression, or what?' She didn't wait for an answer. 'That magazine cover falling through was the luckiest thing that ever happened to you, my dear.'

'I'm inclined to agree,' said Jill.

'I've got a real plum for you. How do you like the idea of the biggest cosmetics firm in the world wanting you to be the representative of their line?'

Jill swallowed hard, and said carefully, 'I think it's a bad joke, Althea.'

'They want a more mature face, for a new line of products. And you're it, Jill. They want you and only you. I've spent all day with them working out the details. We're talking major advertising, television as well as print.'

If all the most wonderful things that have happened to me in the whole eight years of my career were rolled into one, Jill thought, this tops it all.

'It's bigger than anything this agency has done before, let alone any one model, Jill.'

She could see it all: the glamour, the perks, the fame. For an instant, she heard the siren call of success, pulling her back to New York.

But there was also the hard work, the jet-lag, the sacrifices——

She looked up at Scott, at the pain that was reflected in his eyes. He was trying to smile, she saw. Trying to let her go with grace.

The sacrifices, she thought. Funny, what a different meaning that word had now, so unlike what she had thought it meant, just a few hours ago.

'No,' she said. 'I'm not interested.'

There was a tiny shocked silence on the other end of the line. 'You can't be serious, Jill!'

'But I am. Besides, they wouldn't want me now,' Jill added easily. 'I've got three freckles on my nose since I came out here.' She smiled up at Scott.

Althea was nearly shrieking. 'But what are you going to do?'

Jill frowned throughtfully. Then her brow cleared. 'I think I'll go and lie by the pool and acquire a few more,' she announced.

'You're mad,' Althea said flatly. 'Or drunk. In any case, I'll call you tomorrow in the hope that you've got back in touch with reality.'

'Whatever you'd like,' Jill said equably, and hung up while Althea was still talking.

Scott shook his head. 'You're crazy, Jill.'

'That's right. About you,' she whispered.

'To turn that down——'

'There are more important things than having my face plastered across magazine pages. Things like you, and Josh.' She hesitated, and said, very softly, 'Scott, I know I can't ever take Maria's place, but I want so much to try.'

He sighed. 'You don't need to be afraid of my memories of Maria, Jill.'

'I don't resent her,' she said hastily. 'And I know there will be times——'

He put a finger across her lips. 'I did love her,' he said. 'She was—well, she was just Maria, that's all, and there'll never be anyone like her. But I never lied to her, Jill. She knew when she married me that I hadn't finished mourning you and that perhaps I never would.'

She buried her face in his shoulder. It's too much, she thought. All this, and I came so close to throwing it all away because I was too foolish to know what's really important.

'I thought I'd put you behind me,' Scott admitted huskily. 'It was a hell of a shock when you stepped out of that van, Jill, but I thought that what I was feeling was anger, cold fury that you dared to play games with me, after you'd once hurt me so badly. But that first night in the bar I realised that it wasn't over, that it would never be over. That night you were more beautiful than I'd ever seen you before, Jill—with no make-up and your hair wet—the most beautiful you've ever been,' he added softly, 'until I saw you with Josh.'

His hand closed over hers, and she used it to wipe away two fat, hot tears. There was something missing, she thought hazily, and only then did she realise that his wedding ring was gone. She touched the place where it had rested, and looked up at him with a question in her eyes.

'I took it off that night when I got home,' he told her.

'I guess I didn't want to look at it,' Jill admitted unsteadily. 'So I didn't even see that it was gone.'

She didn't know how long Josh might have been standing in the doorway, wide-eyed, before they noticed him. But she felt thoroughly kissed, and she suspected it might have been some time. When she finally did see him, she put her hand over her eyes. Surely, she thought, there were better ways than this of breaking the news to a child. They were being insensitive and cruel——

'Bobby says he guesses this means I'm going to have a new mommy,' Josh announced. 'And he oughta know, because he's had three dads. Is that what it means, Daddy?'

'Yes,' said Scott. 'Any other questions?'

Josh grinned. 'Yeah,' he said. 'When's the spaghetti going to be ready?'

'A long time.' Scott looked down at Jill. 'Why spaghetti, anyway?' he said. 'I thought we were going to have a picnic tonight.'

'Because you said once that it was Josh's favourite. And,' she coloured a little, 'because it was the most fattening thing I could think of, on the spur of the moment.'

'I can see that you're going to be a handful, Mrs Richards.' He kissed her slowly. 'Any doubts, Jill?'

'Not one.' And she knew, as she put her head down on his shoulder again, that as long as he stood beside her she would never want to look back.

EPILOGUE

SLEET rattled against the kitchen windows, and Jill looked up from the skillet full of beef teriyaki with a frown. The store had closed half an hour ago, and Scott wasn't home yet. The baby in her left arm yanked at a lock of Jill's hair and wailed. Jessica had a cold, and life wasn't terribly pleasant for her today. Jill soothed her automatically and turned her attention back to the teriyaki.

Josh came into the kitchen. He was wearing a baseball cap tugged low on his forehead, as if to declare that winter was only a state of mind. 'Mom, Jen's chewing her toes,' he announced.

'She'll be all right,' Jill said absently. 'Wait a minute. She's chewing what?'

'Her toes,' Josh repeated with his best offended-big-brother manner. 'It's really yucky!'

Jill gave him a hug. 'She'll get over it,' she promised. 'And in the meantime, it'll make a good picture.'

The back door banged, and Jill closed her eyes for a moment and sighed in relief. 'Hello, darling,' she said as Scott came into the kitchen. 'Welcome to bedlam.' She kissed him on the cheek and handed him the whimpering baby. 'Please see if you can convince your daughter that her stuffy nose isn't going to be fatal. I'm not having much luck.'

She reached for the camera that had never been out of arm's length since the day the twins had been born. By the time she reached the great room, Jennifer had stopped chewing her toes and started on the corner of her blanket. She obligingly grinned at her mother. 'Cheesecake artist,' Jill accused her, and snapped the shutter.

'Another one for the calendar?' asked Scott. He put Jessica, who was now contentedly sucking her thumb, down beside her sister.

'Possibly. John says I've got nearly enough to choose from. It's been easy enough—these two kids are naturals.'

'How can they be anything else? They were conceived in New York while you were doing the campaign for the cosmetics people,' Scott murmured.

'You don't know that.'

He grinned at her. 'I can count.'

Jill sat back on her heels and said, 'Althea called today. She wants me to do another spread for her. Jewellery this time, for the mature woman,' she mimicked Althea's tone.

'What did you say?'

'That I haven't got back in shape yet after the babies, so I thought I'd better pass.'

'You're in wonderful shape, Jill.'

She shook her head. 'I'm still ten pounds over my shooting weight.' Josh leaned over the twins and crooned softly. Jill snapped a shot of the three of them and put the camera aside.

Scott followed her into the kitchen. 'Taste this,' she demanded. 'I don't think I've got it right yet.'

'Are you sorry, Jill?'

'About the agency? Of course not. I'm glad I did the cosmetics campaign, of course. I wanted to earn the money myself to buy into the studio. But now that I've got a job I love—Cassie's right, you know. Why bother to kill myself losing that last ten pounds? You like me better this way anyway.'

'I like you any way at all, and you know it.'

'Fortunate for me, isn't it?' The words were teasing, but her insides had gone all fuzzy, as they always did when he was near. She smiled up at him.

He rubbed his cheek against her hair. 'Sometimes I wonder, Jill,' he said softly, 'You gave up such a lot, and with the babies coming so much sooner than we'd planned—and two of them, at that——'

'I always did believe in doing things efficiently.'

'You know what I mean. Do you miss it all? Your work? New York?'

Did she miss it? Jill looked around the warm kitchen and thought of Scott, of the babies, of Josh, of the storm outside their snug retreat. Sometimes it seemed that her whole life had happened in the last eighteen months, since she had come to Springhill. Sometimes it felt as if her modelling career had been only a dream, faded and long forgotten and unimportant.

She smiled up at him and rose up on her toes to kiss the cleft in his chin. 'New York?' she said softly. 'Where's that?'

UNPREDICTABLE, COMPELLING AND TOTALLY READABLE

MIDNIGHT JEWELS – *Jayne Ann Krentz*   £2.95

Jayne Ann Krentz, bestselling author of *Crystal Flame*, blends romance and tension in her latest fast-moving novel. An advert for a rare collector's item sparked not only Mercy Pennington's meeting with the formidable Croft Falconer, but also a whole sequence of unpredictable events.

SOMETHING SO RIGHT – *Emilie Richards*   £2.75

The high-flying lifestyle of top recording artist Joelle Lindsay clashed with her attempts to return to her simple roots. This compelling novel of how love conquers disillusionment will captivate you to the last page.

GATHERING PLACE – *Marisa Carroll*   £2.50

Sarah Austin could not confront the future before she had settled her past trauma of having had her child adopted. Her love for Tyler Danielson helped, but she could not understand how his orphaned son seemed so uncannily familiar.

These three new titles will be out in bookshops from July 1989.

W❂RLDWIDE

Available from Boots, Martins, John Menzies, W. H. Smith, Woolworths and other paperback stockists.

COMING SOON FROM MILLS & BOON!

Your chance to win the fabulous

VAUXHALL ASTRA
MERIT 1.2 5-DOOR

Plus

**2000 RUNNER UP PRIZES OF WEEKEND
BREAKS & CLASSIC LOVE SONGS ON CASSETTE**

❤ SEE
MILLS & BOON BOOKS ❤
THROUGHOUT JULY & AUGUST FOR DETAILS

AROUND THE WORLD WORDSEARCH
COMPETITION!

How would you like a years supply of Mills & Boon Romances ABSOLUTELY FREE? Well, you can win them! All you have to do is complete the word puzzle below and send it in to us by October 31st. 1989. The first 5 correct entries picked out of the bag after that date will win **a years supply of Mills & Boon Romances** (*ten books every month - **worth around £150***) What could be easier?

```
R D N A L R E Z T I W S
E O N M C H I N A A C C
G M U I G L E B N N U O
Y E C E G W H I Z C B T
P D R H S E R I A Z A L
T N S M P E R U N D D A
N A W I A T P I I E N N
Y L A T I N A N A N A D
N G S T N H Y D E M L Q
W N O J A M A I C A L A
R E L A D A N A C R O R
T H A I L A N D D K H I
```

ITALY	THAILAND	SCOTLAND	SWITZERLAND
GERMANY	IRAQ	JAMAICA	
HOLLAND	ZAIRE	TANZANIA	
BELGIUM	TAIWAN	PERU	
EGYPT	CANADA	SPAIN	
CHINA	INDIA	DENMARK	
NIGERIA	ENGLAND	CUBA	

PLEASE TURN OVER FOR DETAILS ON HOW TO ENTER

HOW TO ENTER

All the words listed overleaf, below the word puzzle, are hidden in the grid. You can find them by reading the letters forward, backwards, up or down, or diagonally. When you find a word, circle it or put a line through it, the remaining letters (which you can read from left to right, from the top of the puzzle through to the bottom) will spell a secret message.

After you have filled in all the words, don't forget to fill in your name and address in the space provided and pop this page in an envelope (you don't need a stamp) and post it today. Hurry - competition ends October 31st. 1989.

Mills & Boon Competition,
FREEPOST,
P.O. Box 236,
Croydon,
Surrey. CR9 9EL

Only one entry per household

Secret Message _____

_____

Name _____

Address _____

_____

_____

_____ Postcode _____

You may be mailed as a result of entering this competition

COMP 6